The Cupcake Diaries:
Spoonful of Christmas

By Darlene Panzera

Bet You'll Marry Me
The Cupcake Diaries: Sweet on You
The Cupcake Diaries: Recipe for Love
The Cupcake Diaries: Taste of Romance
The Cupcake Diaries: Spoonful of Christmas

The Cupcake Diaries: Spoonful of Christmas

DARLENE PANZERA

AVONIMPULSE
An Imprint of HarperCollinsPublishers

Excerpt from *The Cupcake Diaries: Sweet On You* copyright © 2013 by Darlene Panzera.

Excerpt from *The Cupcake Diaries: Recipe for Love* copyright © 2013 by Darlene Panzera.

Excerpt from *The Cupcake Diaries: Taste of Romance* copyright © 2013 by Darlene Panzera.

Excerpt from *Rescued by a Stranger* copyright © 2013 by Lizbeth Selvig.

Excerpt from *Chasing Morgan* copyright © 2013 by Jennifer Ryan.

Excerpt from *Throwing Heat* copyright © 2013 by Candice Wakoff.

Excerpt from *Private Research* copyright © 2013 by Sabrina Darby.

EPub Edition DECEMBER 2013 ISBN: 9780062305121

Print Edition ISBN: 9780062305145

10 9 8 7 6 5 4 3 2 1

For my husband, Joe, and our children, Samantha, Robert, and Jason, and also for our special cousin Brandi, whom we love so much.

Chapter One

Gifts of time and love are surely the basic ingredients of a truly merry Christmas.

—Peg Bracken

ANDI GLANCED AT the number on the caller ID, picked up the phone, and tried to mimic the deep, sultry voice of a sexy siren. "Hello, Creative Cupcakes."

"What if I told you I'd like to order a Mistletoe Magic cupcake with a dozen delicious kisses on top?"

She smiled at the sound of Jake's voice. "Mistletoe Magic?"

"I was guaranteed that the person who eats it will receive a dozen kisses by midnight."

"What if I told you," Andi said, playing along, "that you don't have to eat a cupcake to get a kiss, and the magic will begin the minute you walk through the front door?"

Jake chuckled. "I'm on my way."

Andi's sister, Kim, and best friend, Rachel, watched her with amused expressions on their faces.

"I hope Mike and I still flirt with each other after *we're* married," Rachel said, her sing-song voice a tease. "But the name 'Mistletoe Magic' isn't half bad. Maybe we *should* make a red velvet cupcake with a Hershey's kiss and miniature holly leaf sprinkles on top."

Kim finished boxing a dozen maraschino cherry cupcakes and handed them to the customer at the counter. "As if we don't have enough sales already."

"Sales are great," Andi agreed. "We've booked orders for eighteen holiday parties. Now, if I can only figure out what to get Jake for Christmas, life would be perfect."

Rachel rang up the next customer's order. "Mike and I decided our Hollywood honeymoon will be our gift to each other."

"Are you serious?" Kim picked up a pastry bag from the back worktable. "You—the woman who can't walk three feet past a store window without buying anything— are not going to get Mike a Christmas gift? Not even a little something?"

"It *is* hard," she admitted. "But I promised him I wouldn't. I also promised I wouldn't go overboard with spending on the wedding arrangements."

"You could always have a small, simple wedding like Jake and I did," Andi suggested.

Rachel's red curls bounced back and forth as she

shook her head. "I already booked the Liberty Theater for the reception. I know it's expensive, but the palace-like antique architecture is so beautiful, I couldn't help myself. I've always dreamed of—"

"Being Cinderella?" Kim joked.

"I *do* want a Cinderella wedding," Rachel crooned. "I figure I can bake my own cake and skimp on other wedding details to stay within our budget."

Andi didn't think Rachel knew the first thing about staying within a budget but decided it was best not to argue. Instead, she turned toward her younger sister. "Kim, what are you getting Nathaniel for Christmas?"

"I'm not sure." Kim shrugged away. "Maybe I should just get him a new set of luggage tags."

Rachel frowned. "That's not very romantic."

"No, but it's practical," Andi said, coming to Kim's defense. "Nathaniel's probably getting her the same thing."

"He planned to fly to his family's home in Sweden this Christmas," Kim confessed, her dark eyebrows drawing together. "But I told him I couldn't go, and he didn't want to go without me."

"Of course you can't go!" Rachel said, bracing her hands against the marble counter. "I need you to be my bridesmaid!"

"It would have been awkward spending Christmas with his family anyway," Kim said, as she piped vanilla icing over the cupcakes. "It's not like I'm part of his family or like we're even engaged. In fact, I don't know what we are."

"You two are great together," Andi encouraged. "You are both artistic, enjoy nature, and love to travel."

Kim nodded, then looked up, her expression earnest. "But what else? I'm beginning to wonder if I should tell Nathaniel to go to Sweden without me."

"And miss my wedding? But you'll need a dance partner at the reception," Rachel reminded her. "He wouldn't go and leave you stranded without a date on Christmas Eve, would he?"

Kim hesitated. "I don't know."

The bells on the front door jingled as a man in his late forties wearing a pricey three-piece business suit entered the shop with a briefcase in hand.

"Are you the owners of Creative Cupcakes?" he asked, his expression hopeful.

Andi stepped forward and smiled. "Yes, we are."

"I'm Preston Pennyworth." He placed his briefcase on the end of the counter and released the latch. "And I have an offer I think you might like."

"What kind of offer?" Rachel asked, anticipation lighting her faint-freckled face.

Mr. Pennyworth handed them each a set of papers a half-inch thick. "An offer to buy Creative Cupcakes."

Thirty minutes later, after the businessman had left, Andi, Rachel, and Kim sat staring at the pink-swirled, strawberry parfait cupcake they'd placed at the center of the table for Rachel's birthday.

"I can't believe that just happened," Andi said, breaking the silence.

"A million dollars is a lot of money," Rachel commented.

"Enough for *each* of us to start our own businesses," Kim added.

Andi picked up the long golden cupcake cutter they'd bought to celebrate the grand opening of Creative Cupcakes and held it tight in her hand. "The fact we own the property is a huge plus. And our revenue from shipping cupcakes and packaged mixes nationwide has increased every month, making our shop very attractive to prospective buyers." She paused. "But, of course, we'd never sell to him or anyone else who offered."

"No," Rachel chorused. "Of course not."

"Even though I could travel to every art gallery around the world," Kim said dreamily. "Or buy my own art gallery to house all my paintings."

Rachel gasped. "I could have the wedding of the century."

"I could put a down payment on a big house with twenty bedrooms," Andi told them. "A master suite for me and Jake, a bedroom for each of the girls, and—"

"What would you do with the other seventeen bedrooms?" Rachel demanded.

"I'd use them as guest rooms."

Kim laughed. "Sounds like a hotel, but knowing you, you'd probably invite every homeless person on the street into the house for the night."

"Imagine how many people I could help," Andi countered. "I'd be doing a good deed."

"Speaking of good deeds," Rachel said, nodding to the cupcake cutter in her hand, "are you going to split that cupcake?"

Andi divided Rachel's birthday cupcake into threes and served them each a piece on a napkin, as was their tradition. In the past they'd divided the cupcake to cut calories, and this year was no exception. They had only five weeks before they had to squeeze into their slinky designer dresses for Rachel's wedding.

Because their birthdays were spaced four months apart, they also set goals for themselves from one person's birthday to the next—which, of course, was much easier than setting goals for a whole year.

As usual, Andi had an ever-growing list of goals, but her first one was to tell her husband about Preston Pennyworth's outrageous offer.

AN HOUR LATER Andi met Jake for lunch at the Captain's Port, the restaurant where they had first met. Out the window, a seal bobbed up and down in the wake left behind from the large cargo vessels making their way down the Columbia River toward the Pacific Ocean.

Andi bobbed up and down in her seat as well, anxious to see Jake's reaction to the news she just gave him.

"He offered to buy Creative Cupcakes for *a million dollars*?" Jake's eyebrows shot upward. "What did you tell him?"

Andi laughed. "First our jaws hit the floor from shock. Then I let Mr. Pennyworth know how hard we had worked to make the shop a success. And you know what he did? He upped his offer to *one-point-two* million."

"That's twice what it's worth."

"Pennyworth said his daughter has a dream to own a cupcake shop, and he's determined to buy her one, no matter what the cost. They love our view of the Astoria-Megler Bridge through our shop windows and have made it clear they don't want to be rivals with us."

"Of course not. We'd put them out of business."

"*That's* why they want to buy us out and then open other stores across the country using our name and logo."

Jake let out a soft whistle, obviously impressed.

"They said if they bought Creative Cupcakes, they'd also want rights to the recipes," Andi continued, then scowled. "The recipes handed down to me from my mother."

The expression on Jake's face seemed more hesitant than sympathetic—not what she had expected.

"You turned him down, didn't you?" he asked.

"Of course I turned him down. I wouldn't sell the shop for any amount of money. Would you?"

He'd won her over with his whole-hearted support of the cupcake shop earlier that year. Since then, he'd become her business partner, her husband, and a father to her six-year-old daughter, Mia. So why was he looking at her as if he were unsure what to say?

Andi frowned, then repeated the question. "Would you sell Creative Cupcakes?"

Jake cleared his throat. "I think we should leave all options on the table until we've had a chance to discuss the matter."

Andi longed to brush the light brown hair off his forehead and check his temperature to see if he was feeling okay, because at the moment he didn't sound anything like the man she had fallen in love with. "What is there to discuss?"

"I have news for you, too," Jake said, reaching across the table to take her hand.

Oh-oh. She didn't like the shadow in his eyes or the ominous tone in his voice.

"Something . . . good?" she ventured.

"I've been offered a job—in Washington—as a staff reporter," he said quickly. "It's a big step up with a double pay raise, but—"

"Oh, Jake!" Andi gushed, her anxiety slipping away. "That's fantastic! But I'm not surprised. Your articles for the *Astoria Sun* have been gaining national recognition."

Jake flashed her a big smile. "I've always dreamed of an opportunity like this, but I never thought in a million years they'd contact *me* . . . or that you would be okay with it."

"Why wouldn't I be okay with it? The commute shouldn't be too bad. Washington is just over the bridge."

Jake's smile faded. "Not Washington State, Andi."

"No?" The back of her throat closed. *He couldn't possibly mean—*

"Washington, D.C." he affirmed. "I'd be working for the *Washington Post*."

Her jaw dropped for the second time that day, and for a moment she couldn't breathe. "Th-that's the other side of the country."

Jake pulled her hand to his mouth for a quick kiss. "I know. We'd have to move. But just think—you could branch out, open a second cupcake shop there, create your own nationwide chain of stores."

"Leave Rachel and Kim?" Andi's heart slammed against her ribs with a jolt that was downright painful.

Then she looked at the eager expression on Jake's face and realized her own dreams of opening the cupcake shop would never have come to fruition if it weren't for his support. Now—especially as his wife—shouldn't she return the favor and support his dreams, too?

"I told the senior editor I had a family and would need to discuss the offer with you," Jake told her. "But he'd like a decision by the first of the year."

Andi thought of her first marriage and how badly it had ended—with her deadbeat husband running off and leaving her to support Mia on her own. She'd been blessed to meet Jake, who had lost his wife to cancer and was also a single parent.

But could she pick up and move away from the rest of her family and friends, the people with whom she'd spent her whole life? She'd never lived outside Astoria, Oregon. It was all she knew. And unlike her adventurous sister, Kim, it was all she had ever cared to know.

"Promise me you'll think about it?" Jake asked.

Andi swallowed hard and nodded. "I will."

Chapter Two

Blessed is the season which engages the whole world in a conspiracy of love!

—Hamilton Wright Mabie

RACHEL SPUN AROUND in front of the mirror, the skirt of her white fairytale wedding gown swishing past the others' knees in the crowded back bedroom of her mother's house.

"What do you think?" she asked, giving them a big smile as she turned first this way and then the other.

"You look fat," Kim teased.

"I do not!" she said, scrunching her face. "Except for Thanksgiving dinner, I've been eating nothing but salad for two whole weeks."

"You're beautiful," Andi affirmed. She held still while

Rachel's mother, Sarah, stuck pins into the hem of her holly green bridesmaid dress. "Mike will be mesmerized the moment he sees you walk down the aisle."

"Don't you mean hypnotized?" Sarah joked, as she pulled a loose thread off her daughter's sleeve. "Like the poor souls who fall victim to his magic tricks?"

"I think he's the one who must have hypnotized Rachel to convince her to break her two-date-only rule and marry him so fast," Andi said, breaking into a grin.

"Mike's too busy driving the Cupcake Mobile and working on his miniature models for the movie studios to perform any magic tricks these days," Rachel informed them.

"What about when he kisses you?" Kim asked, her face etched with mock innocence. "Didn't you tell us his kisses were magical?"

"One of a kind," Rachel agreed. "Mom, when will the bridesmaid dresses be finished?"

"Unless something goes wrong, I'll have them stitched together and hemmed next week."

"Nothing can go wrong," Rachel said, twirling in front of the mirror again.

"I hope you're right," Andi said, looping an arm around her shoulders. "But not everything always goes as planned. Remember how it rained on my wedding day back in September?"

Rachel nodded. Andi's wedding had been full of last-minute changes due to the weather. The ceremony, set to take place on the waterfront dock, had to be moved to an inside pavilion. Jake's daughter, Taylor, and Andi's daughter, Mia, both six, soaked the fancy shoes dyed to match their dresses when they jumped in a puddle. And the umbrella's donated last minute by the Fish 'N' Nets cafe for the bridal party were imprinted with tiny dancing shrimp.

Andi and Jake had been so much in love that none of it mattered to them. But Rachel couldn't fathom what she'd do if something like that happened to her.

She wanted *her* wedding to be perfect.

KIMBERLY NICOLE BURKE dipped a paintbrush into the can of green paint she'd perched on the top of the ladder. Then, using broad, sweeping strokes she created the branches of an evergreen tree on the glass of the large six-by-six shop window. A small dab of blue on the snowman's button, a red swirl on the lollipop sticking out of the stocking, and there! Her window decorations were finished.

She was leaning back to admire her work when Andi came out the front door, bundled in her coat, carrying a coiled strand of multicolored Christmas lights.

"Ready for these?" Andi asked, lifting the bundle of bulbs up to her.

Kim nodded. "I want to decorate the whole shop and have a good old-fashioned Christmas like we did when Mom was still with us."

"That would be nice," Andi said, her voice soft. "You never know when it might be our last Christmas together."

Kim thought of Nathaniel, his blond hair, his Swedish accent, his cute, quirky ways. Before she met him, she'd spent several years alone. And if he wasn't as committed as she was to their relationship, she might be alone again by this time next year.

"*Ja*," Kim said, mimicking his lilting Scandinavian tone. "You never know."

"Careful you don't fall off the ladder," Andi warned.

Kim laughed. "After I've flown to Sweden, bungee jumped in Italy, hiked to the top of Mount Hood, and parasailed in the Bahamas, you're worried about me falling off a *ladder*?"

Rachel came out the front door, carrying an air pump and a blow-up Frosty the Snowman. "That's Andi for you, always worrying about everyone's safety."

"You have to admit, I'm not nearly as OCD as I used to be." Andi smiled to herself. "Especially now that I'm married to Jake."

"Yeah, Jake has had a calming effect on you," Kim replied. "Except for the past week or two. Are you fighting?"

Andi jerked her head backward. "Of course not. We've just been busy. First we had Rachel's birthday and then Thanksgiving. Now we're decorating for Christmas, and I still need to shop—"

Both Andi and the "I'll Be Home for Christmas" carol playing on Kim's portable radio were disrupted by the rattling, tinkering sound of the Cupcake Mobile turning the corner. The 1933 antique bread-loaf-shaped truck parked next to the curb, and Mike Palmer climbed out, followed by Nathaniel Sjölander.

"They got the tree!" Kim climbed down the ladder and hurried to Nathaniel's side. "Smells fresh."

"We cut it down less than fifteen minutes ago. The best tree in my nursery," Nathaniel said as he helped Mike carry the blue spruce toward the front door.

"Sjölander's is the best." Kim's heart swelled as she thought of all the wonderful flowers she'd received over the past year as a result of dating the owner. "Your brother didn't mind running the business and tending to the gardens while we were off on our adventures?"

Nathaniel slid her a quick glance. "Well, no, but Fredrik's glad we're back."

Kim was glad, too. Her dream of having her passport filled with stamps was great, but she'd missed her friends and family—and being a regular part of the cupcake shop.

She never thought she'd say this, but this year she looked forward to spending the holidays . . . at *home*.

"Ow!" MAX HOLLOWAY raised the hem of the white, floor-length tablecloth and stuck his head out. "You kicked me!"

A young girl with blond hair and enormous blue eyes peered down at him. "What are you doing under the table?"

"None of your business."

"You need a haircut."

Max swiped a long strand of his shaggy brown hair out of his eyes. "That's none of your business either."

"How old are you?"

Max scowled, wishing he'd kept his location a secret. "Twelve. And I don't talk to little kids."

"I'm not little," the girl shot back. "I go to school all day now. I'm in the first grade."

"You are, too, little," he argued. "Go away."

She lifted her chin. "This is my snack spot."

Max glanced at the brown paper lunch bag in her hands and thought he could smell peanut butter. "What kind of snacks do you have?"

The girl raised the bag out of his reach. "What's your name?"

He could also smell some kind of fruit candy, and his mouth started to water. Maybe he could convince her to give him some. *If he was nice.*

"Max." He glanced around the interior of the shop to make sure no one else had spotted him. "My name is Max."

"I used to have a dog named Max. He's gone now. I'm Mia." The first-grader opened the bag and dug in. "Do you want some crackers?"

Max snatched the peanut butter sandwich crackers from her hands. "Yeah, thanks."

"Why are you hiding?"

Max ripped open the plastic wrapper holding his treat. "I'm not hiding, I just want to be alone."

"I hid from my mom once, but she found me. Where's your mom?"

Max shoved the crackers into his mouth, wishing Mia would stop asking him so many questions. "I don't have a mom."

"What about a dad?"

Now she was bothering him. "I don't have a dad."

Mia leaned her head closer. "Who packs your lunch-box for school?"

"I have foster parents," Max said, motioning toward the brown bag for another treat. "But they don't care about me."

Mia waved an open bag of Gummy Bears in front of his face. "Why not?"

Max tried to reach for the candy, but Mia pulled it away and giggled. Frustrated, he replied, "They just don't."

Her eyes widened. "Were you bad?"

"No! I'm just not—theirs. All they care about is the money they get for giving me a place to stay. They fight all the time. I think they're going to get a divorce."

"My mom got a divorce," she said and handed him the fruit-scented Gummy Bears. "Then she married Jake. Now he's my dad."

Mia pointed to the front of the cupcake counter, where a woman in an apron waved a wooden spoon at a guy with a newspaper tucked under the arm of his blue sport jacket. "There they are."

Max watched the couple as they drew toward each other for a hug. "Do you ever see your real dad?"

Mia frowned, as if confused. "I was like you. I didn't have a real dad until Jake."

"Do you like him?"

She laughed. "Of course. Jake's fun."

Fun? *Yeah, right.* Not possible. He'd never known *any*

parent to be fun. But what did Mia know? She was just a child. He'd even bet his At Athens Alone drumstick the girl still believed in Santa Claus.

"How is my lovely wife today?" Jake asked, taking the wooden spoon from her hand and setting it on the counter.

"Mrs. Hartman is busy," Andi said, and tried to turn away from him.

It didn't work. Jake stretched his arms around her from behind and covered her eyes with his hands. "I have a surprise for you. In the kitchen. Just walk forward, and I'll guide you."

Okay, she *did* love surprises—as long as they were good. She heard the double doors open and then Jake's voice telling their three college-age employee's to man the front of the shop for a few minutes. Their footsteps shuffled past her as Jake's strong arms led her a few more feet. Then they came to a stop, and a mixture of cream cheese frosting and pine assaulted her nose.

"Okay, open them."

Andi opened her eyes and looked up. A sprig of mistletoe hung from the ceiling overhead. "Mistletoe Magic?"

Jake kissed her, and images of the first time she met him floated in her mind. She'd run all over town searching for a cupcake for Kim's birthday when she found one in Jake's possession at the Captain's Port. However, convincing him to let her have it wasn't "a piece of cake." She'd thought she might have to shanghai him to get her hands on the treat.

The Captain's Port was famous for the trapdoor through which drunken customers in the past had often been shanghaied into becoming crew members at sea. For a brief moment, she had entertained the notion of shoving Jake down the hatch and refusing to let him out until he said the cupcake was hers. But in the end she hadn't had to use such drastic means. He'd agreed to split the cupcake with her. And thus began their romance.

Jake pulled his mouth away and kissed her on the end of her nose. "I'm sorry, Andi. I'm a better writer than I am a speaker, and I shouldn't have worded the news about my job offer in D.C. that way. Nothing is set in stone. You know I won't take the job if you don't want me to."

"I'm sorry, too," Andi admitted. "The way I've been avoiding you is unfair. I've only been thinking of myself. And I don't want anything to ruin our first Christmas together."

Jake kissed her again. "I don't either. Have you told Rachel and Kim?"

Andi shook her head. "Not until we make a final decision. But, Jake, can't we wait until *after* Christmas?"

"Of course," Jake agreed. "If we decide to move, we don't want to upset Rachel before her wedding, or upset Kim and the girls. I hadn't thought about Mia's and Taylor's reactions."

Andi walked over to the cupcake tray rack and brought Jake one of her newest creations. "I baked these this morning."

Jake took a bite of the red velvet cupcake set in the candy cane-printed wrapper, iced with white icing and topped with a Hershey's kiss and a green sprig of mint candy. "Mistletoe Magic cupcakes?"

Andi smiled. "You gave me the idea. Everyone says they 'taste as good as a kiss.'"

Jake pulled her against him with his free arm. "Close. But I still think a real kiss from you is better."

He drew his mouth toward her again, and Andi melted into him, glad Jake brought her into the privacy of the kitchen.

"I love you, Jake."

"I love you, too, Andi."

"I won't let anything ruin this Christmas," she promised.

"I won't either," Jake vowed. "Let's make this the best Christmas we've ever had."

Andi gave him a big smile. "Sounds like a plan."

THE NEXT MORNING when Andi got out of her car, she noticed that the snowman Rachel had inflated outside the shop the day before lay in a heap on the ground. Maybe it had a leak?

But as she drew closer, she also saw that the beautiful wreath with pinecones and shiny gold balls that Nathaniel had put on the front door was also missing.

Worse, Rachel stood in front of the Creative Cupcakes window tossing her head like a red bull. Kim, the least likely one to show emotion, waved her clenched fists in the air.

"What's wrong?" Andi asked, quickening her pace as she made her way to them.

"Creative Cupcakes has been vandalized!" Rachel exclaimed.

Andi gasped. "What!"

Rachel and Kim stepped away from the window, and instead of Kim's pretty paintings, a new image decorated the glass.

A big, hairy, green, sharp-toothed Grinch.

Chapter Three

He who has not Christmas in his heart will never find it under a tree.

—Roy L. Smith

ANDI STARED AT the green monster, wishing it were a weekday when Mia and Taylor were in school, but being a Saturday, they were right behind her.

"Grinch!" Taylor cried. "I'm scared of the Grinch!"

Taylor hugged Andi's legs, almost tripping her. But Mia drew closer to the storefront wreckage.

"The Grinch hurt Frosty," Mia said, pointing to the pile of white vinyl.

Andi glanced at the doorknob, where a long string of jingle bells had dangled, and the top of the window, where they had strung Christmas lights. What did the thief do with them?

"If I catch whoever did this," Andi growled, "I'm going to wring his little neck."

"Not if I get to him first," Kim said. "He painted over everything I did yesterday."

Rachel pursed her lips. "You have to admit the vandal is a pretty good artist. Although whoever did this got his Christmas stories crossed."

"What do you mean?" Mia asked, coming over to investigate.

"See the words painted beneath the face of the Grinch?" Rachel explained, tapping her fingernails against the glass. "'Bah humbug' is a famous saying from *A Christmas Carol*, you know, the story about Scrooge."

Kim bent toward the Grinch and looked more closely. "Looks like he started to use spray paint but then switched over to brushes."

Andi went and stood next to her and studied the artwork. "Why would he do that?"

"He's angry," Kim assured her, "but notice the intricate brushstroke design, the detail he put into the facial expression? I think deep down inside, he's also an artist who cares about his work."

Andi frowned. "At least he cares about *something*."

"So there's still hope for him?" Mia asked, turning to face her.

Andi nodded. "There's always hope."

WHEN OFFICER IAN Lockwell arrived at the shop, he helped Andi review the security camera footage shot the night before. Unfortunately the lens faced into the shop and not toward the outside.

"I don't understand," Andi grumbled. "Why would anyone do this?"

Mia stopped taping red and green strips of paper into a chain to answer her. "Because his heart is too small."

Rachel laughed. "Yes, in the story the Grinch needed a bigger heart."

Andi pulled out a new three-ring binder decorated with flying reindeer—which Mia had picked out—and spread it open on the front counter.

"Our new Cupcake Diary," she announced.

On page 1 she had recorded the recipe for Mistletoe Magic cupcakes. Taking a pen, she wrote on page 2, *How to catch a Grinch.*

"A trap?" Rachel suggested.

"Another security camera?" Kim offered.

Mia shook her blond braids back and forth. "*Love.* Didn't you see the cartoon on TV? You have to catch the Grinch with love."

Ian chuckled. "How do you do that?"

"I'm going to make him a present," Mia declared.

Andi exchanged smiles with Rachel and Kim as Mia took out her crayons and began to color a picture.

"I'm going to make a present for Max, too," Mia added.

"Who's Max?" Andi inquired.

"He's the boy under the table."

Andi glanced at Taylor. "Did you see a boy?"

Taylor shook her head, and Andi bit her lip.

After her divorce, Mia had been upset and developed an imaginary friend to help her deal with her emotions. Was this Mia's way of covering her fear of the vandalism?

Mia's eighteen-year-old babysitter, Heather, who doubled as one of their employees, walked through the front door. "Sorry I'm late for work. Traffic was terrible. Everyone's Christmas shopping."

Guy Armstrong, the white-ponytailed tattoo artist from the building next door, entered the shop behind her. "Carolers are strolling the streets singing and carrying on about glad tidings of joy and whatever. I'll be glad when the whole holiday season is behind us."

"What's the matter, Guy?" Kim teased. "Don't you like Christmas?"

"No, I don't. It's all a bunch of commercial nonsense, everyone spending all their hard-earned money on gifts they don't even need. And there's no sense putting up a tree and making a fuss when I'm all alone."

Mia's mouth popped open. "Guy, are you the Grinch?"

Guy laughed. "No, and I'm not Santa Claus either."

Mia made a face. "I know that. Of course you aren't Santa. You're silly, Guy."

"So now I'm a silly guy?" he joked.

"No," Andi told him, as she took one of her newest baked treats out of the glass display case and handed it to him. "You're just in desperate need of a Mistletoe Magic cupcake. And we're in desperate need of another set of eyes on our shop at night."

"Sure," Guy agreed. "What am I looking for?"

Andi smiled. "Anyone who wants to steal Christmas."

RACHEL DIDN'T REALIZE Mike had come up behind her in the kitchen until he pulled the long scroll of yellow notepaper out of her hands.

"Are you making a list and checking it twice?" he teased.

"You aren't supposed to see!" she squealed as she tried to get the paper back.

"Why not?" Mike grinned. "There shouldn't be anything for me on there since we agreed not to get each other Christmas gifts this year, right?"

Rachel hesitated. "A fun gift under five dollars wouldn't count, would it?"

Mike frowned. "Rachel—"

"Okay, okay, no gifts," she agreed. "There's no extra money anyway. Mike, I think we've made a mistake. We should never have decided to get married on Christmas Eve."

A look of uncertainty flashed across his face. "Are you having second thoughts?"

"Not about marrying *you*," Rachel amended. "But about the date. I didn't realize we'd have to budget money for the wedding *and* Christmas at the same time."

"We could elope."

"Mike, I'm serious."

"So am I. If we skip out of town, you won't have to worry about your crazy cousin Stacey ruining the wedding."

"Good point," she said and grinned. "But my mother spent countless hours sewing my wedding dress, not to mention the dresses of my bridesmaids, and she wants the whole town to see. Besides, that doesn't solve our dilemma over Christmas gifts. What are we going to get Grandpa Lewy?"

"Easy. All he ever wants is cupcakes."

"We can't give *everyone* cupcakes for Christmas."

"Why not?"

Rachel laughed. "All right. Cupcakes it is."

Mike pulled her into his arms, glanced up at the mistletoe hanging above them, and gave her a warm kiss. "Selling 'Cupcakes' to that businessman would be the only other way to pay for everything on your list."

"If it were up to me," Rachel whispered, her eyes on the double doors of the kitchen, "I'd take the money and run."

"You would?" Mike asked, surprised. "I would, too."

"You think we should accept the offer?"

"Yeah, but it's not *my* business, so I wasn't going to say anything."

Rachel winced. "But how do I tell Andi?"

"You could stick a note into the Cupcake Diary," Mike suggested.

"Andi would *kill me*. She's got her heart set on keeping Creative Cupcakes, and together, she and Jake own half the shop's business shares."

"One-fourth of one-point-two million is three hundred thousand." Mike gave her a mischievous grin. "With my salary and the extra money, we could move to Hollywood, closer to the studios I work for, and you wouldn't have to work at all."

"What *would* I do?" She pursed her lips as she considered. "Get my nails done? Shop for new furniture? Audition for a TV commercial?"

"We could start a family." Mike brushed the side of her face with his finger. "Wouldn't you like to be a mom?"

"I—I don't know. I'd like to concentrate on the wedding first. You know, make sure I don't trip down the aisle in my high heels and fall flat on my face."

"If you trip, I'll catch you," Mike promised. "You know I will always be there for you."

Even if she didn't want kids right away? She loved Mia and had recently gotten to know Taylor, but she'd never done much babysitting. And changing dirty diapers was not her idea of fun.

Maybe it was a good thing Andi wanted to keep the shop. While money would be nice, she wasn't sure she was in sync with Mike's idea of what they should do with it.

KIM PICKED UP one of the green wreaths piled around the greenhouse at Sjölander's Nursery and breathed in the strong, fresh pine scent. "I love the smell of Christmas."

"I have over one hundred wreaths if you have the urge to sniff them all," Nathaniel teased, reminding her of the day they met.

She'd mistaken his backyard for the local park and had vowed to sniff one hundred roses, one for every item on her to-do list. "No, I can smell them all from right here."

Nathaniel finished tying the last of the red velvet bows on the wreaths he'd put together that night, then handed her a box wrapped in brown paper from his table. The stamps on it indicated it was from Sweden.

"My sister sent you a Christmas gift," Nathaniel told her. "Go ahead, open it."

Kim had made friends with Nathaniel's sister, Linnea, when they visited his family two months before. His mother, however, still held a grudge against Kim for smashing the beautiful cupcakes at Fredrik and his bride Maria's Astoria wedding. The forbidding woman didn't understand that she'd had to find Andi's engagement ring, which had fallen into the batter during preparation.

"*God Jul . . . Och Ett Gott Nytt Ar!*" Kim read off the gift tag. "What does it mean?"

Nathaniel grinned. "Merry Christmas . . . and a Happy New Year."

She tore off the brown paper, then opened the box and lifted the gift from its soft tissue wrapping. A small round plate held four white taper candles. In the very middle was a mobile of bells and angels.

"Angel chimes," Nathaniel explained. "A traditional Scandinavian holiday decoration."

"It's beautiful," Kim said, appreciating the intricate detail.

"Let me show you how it works." Nathaniel took a

lighter from his pocket and lit the candles. "The heat from the candles spins the top, causing the angels to tap the bells."

Kim watched the metal angel cutouts turn under the small bells and listened to the tinkling sound they made. "All the angels are shown blowing horns."

"The chimes symbolize the noise of the heavenly host trumpeting the news of the Christ child's birth to the shepherds."

"This is wonderful," Kim told him. "I'll call your sister to thank her. But—"

"But what?" he asked, sitting down on a wooden crate beside her.

"Don't you want to fly home for Christmas? Without me?"

"My family understands you are in a wedding and that I want to be with you." He stood up and wrapped his arms around her, then gave her a hug. "I thought we could go to Sweden for New Year's."

"Rachel will be away on her honeymoon," Kim said, shaking her head. "I'll need to stay and help Andi run the shop."

"What if I buy tickets for the week after?"

"Is that what you plan to get me for Christmas? Tickets?"

Nathaniel pulled back to look at her. "Is that what you want?"

Kim's throat tightened. Why was it so hard to explain to him what she was feeling? Instead, she asked, "What do *you* want? For *us*?"

Nathaniel laughed. "I want to travel the world . . . with you for a whole year straight."

"Didn't we already travel the world these past six months?"

"There's so much more to see and do and experience."

"We'd never be able to afford such a trip."

"You'd never leave the shop for that long, unless . . ." He grinned.

"Unless?" she prompted.

"Not unless we sold both our businesses," Nathaniel said. He gave her an expectant look. "Can you imagine?"

Kim shook her head. "No, I can't. You know I love to travel, but lately . . . I'm longing for more."

"Like an underwater dive into the canyons of the deep?" he suggested.

Kim frowned. "No."

"Or like a rocket ship ride to the moon?"

He laughed, and she realized he was teasing her. She smiled back. "No. I had something different in mind."

"How about one hundred kisses?" he asked, drawing his face near.

"Only a hundred?"

She expected him to close the distance between his mouth and hers, but instead he whispered, his tone serious, "What do *you* want for us, Kimberly?"

She hesitated, unable to conjure up the courage to tell him for fear he'd break up with her. And she couldn't lose him. Not before Christmas.

"One hundred kisses sounds perfect," she replied. *For now.*

Chapter Four

Christmas is not as much about opening our
presents as opening our hearts.

—Janice Maeditere

MAX SPOTTED A man in a blue sport jacket knocking on
the door of the square, white, one-story cottage he shared
with his foster parents and skidded the rusted bicycle
he'd borrowed to a stop.

"There's no one home," Max called over to him. "They
left this morning."

The man turned around, and Max sucked in his
breath. It was Mia's new stepdad, the one she'd pointed
out at the cupcake shop.

"Do you know them? Mr. and Mrs. Gilmore?" the
man asked, walking toward him.

"Yeah." Max stiffened as Mia's step-dad drew closer. Should he take off on the bike and lose him? But why was the guy here? What was going on? Maybe he should stick around a few minutes and find out.

"I'm Jake Hartman," the man said, "A reporter for the *Astoria Sun*. I was told I could interview the Gilmores today."

Max shrugged. "What for?"

The reporter seemed to eye him suspiciously, as if taking in every detail of his appearance to write about *him*. Max didn't like it. Better to split now, while he still had the chance.

But when he went to kick the pedal up on the rusted piece of junk, Jake put his hand on the handlebar, locking it in place. "I'm interviewing foster care families for an upcoming holiday article. Do you know the foster kid who lives at that house?"

"Nope."

Jake glanced at the notepad in his hand. "I was told they had a boy."

"One too many," Max scoffed. "I hear the Gilmores never see him."

Jake frowned. "But they're responsible for him."

"Yeah." Max grinned and shook his head. "Responsible for putting a roof over his head, but that's about it."

"What do you mean?"

Max hesitated. He'd said too much already. "Some foster parents take kids in for the money the state gives them."

"The state gives money to help buy clothes, food, and

other necessary items to raise and support the children," Jake explained.

Max couldn't help but smirk. "Yeah, right."

Jake studied him again, and Max could almost read his thoughts. The guy was thinking that he needed a haircut, a bath, a new pair of shoes without holes, jeans, too, and maybe even a coat because it was cold outside. Any minute he was going to make a comment on his appearance, any second. Then he was going to ask why he wasn't in school.

"What's that in your back pocket?" Jake asked, motioning behind him.

"Huh?" For a moment Max was thrown off guard, then he pulled out his drumstick. "I got it from a local band."

"At Athens Alone?" Jake sounded impressed. "I wrote an article about them a couple months ago. They have a great sound."

What did *he* know about music? He was probably just saying that to get him to talk more about his foster parents.

"My next stop is the music store on Commercial Street," Jake told him. "My buddy owns the place. Would you like to tag along and play on a real drum set?"

Max hesitated again. "No strings attached?"

"No strings attached," Jake assured him.

What was with this guy? Why would he offer him something like that? No one ever offered him anything; most times they just wanted to take things away. But he'd been around people who looked a whole lot more threatening than a clean-cut newspaper reporter in an expensive jacket. And Mia hadn't been afraid of him. She said he was fun. Even if he wasn't, there was no harm going to a public place.

"Okay," Max agreed. "I'll follow you on my bike."

Commercial Street was only a few blocks away. Mia's stepdad drove his car slowly and came to a stop outside Larry's Music Center. Max still wasn't sure what Jake was up to, but he wasn't about to give up the chance to play on a real drum set. And after a quick word with the owner, Jake kept his promise.

The owner led Max to a room in the back, a studio used for recording. Wow! A Pearl drum set stood in the middle, with three types of cymbals—two crashes, a ride, and a hi-hat. The set also had a bass drum, a snare, two toms, and a floor tom. Max slid onto the stool, his heart racing.

"You're going to need two drumsticks to play," Jake said, handing him another to go with the one he had. Then he picked up an electric guitar and put the strap around his neck. The owner of the store held a bass guitar and plugged a cord into the PA system.

"What are you doing?" Max asked, unable to mask his alarm.

"We're going to jam with you," Jake said with a grin. "Is that okay?"

Jam? Like a real band? Max narrowed his eyes. "Do you know how to play?"

Jake laughed. "Do *you*?"

Max tested the set, drumming as fast as he remembered how. It had been a long time since he'd played a real set. Eight months. And that had only been for a short time. A friend at school had offered to teach him, but then Child Protective Services sent him off to live with the Gilmores.

"Not bad," Jake encouraged. "With some lessons, you'd be a real pro."

"That's the plan," Max said, and ran his drumsticks over the series of drums again. "I'm going to be in a rock band, play at shows, and make a ton of money."

"And what would you do with that money?" Jake asked, not looking at him, but tuning his guitar.

"I'd . . ." Max didn't have an answer. His first thought was that he'd find his mother. But he didn't know where she was and doubted money would make a difference. "I guess I'd . . . have a good time."

"Let's see if we can have a good time now," Jake said and nodded to his music store friend. "Ready?"

MAX HAD NEVER jammed with old people before, but for a couple of guys in their thirties, Jake and his friend weren't half bad. And the drum set they'd allowed him to play was *awesome,* so awesome he was quick to express his thanks.

"Anytime," the store owner replied.

Max thanked Mia's stepdad, too. Mia was right; Jake *was* fun. And he didn't hound him with stupid questions. Max took a step toward his bike, wishing he didn't have to go back.

"Hey, Max," Jake called and stuck a thumb toward the restaurant on the corner. "Are you hungry?"

Starving. Okay, maybe he could hang with the old guy a little longer. At least until after lunch.

Max grinned, his mouth already watering from the smell of charbroiled hamburgers and French fries. "You buying?"

ANDI SWAYED HER hips as she danced around the kitchen of Creative Cupcakes to "Rudolph the Red-Nosed Reindeer," "Jingle Bell Rock," and now, her personal favorite—"Home for the Holidays."

She measured out a spoonful of sugar into one bowl, a spoonful of lemon extract into another, and a spoonful of almond cream into a third. Then she took a tray of gingerbread molasses cupcakes out of the oven, slid it onto one of the multilevel wire racks to cool, and carried another tray through the double doors to the front counter.

"I've got the phone," Rachel called, as it rang for the millionth time that afternoon. "A dozen sugarplum cupcakes?"

Two of their college employees, Heather and Theresa, whisked past in their new, bright red aprons, which had been ordered for the Christmas season.

"Coming through with a batch of cinnamon spice," Theresa warned, carrying the tray to the back table, where Kim was decorating with fondant and different colored food gels.

Behind Andi, the double doors to the kitchen re-opened, and Eric, their third college-age employee, poked his head out. "Where's Mike with the Cupcake Mobile? I've boxed up ten more orders ready for delivery."

"He'll be back soon," Rachel informed him, hanging up the phone. "Make sure the packaged mixes of brandy butter-cream frosting are ready to be dropped off for shipping."

"Andi," Heather said, "there's a customer to see you."

She put down the tray of rum ball cupcakes she intended to load into the glass display case and approached the elderly lady who waited for her. "Bernice! How are you?"

"Rachel's busy, so I wanted to give you this," she said, handing her a box wrapped in Santa print Christmas paper. "It's from me and Rachel's grandpa Lewy."

"A gift?" Andi took out the ceramic cupcake-shaped frame with a picture of Rachel, Kim, and her inside. In the photo they were wearing pink bandanas over their hair and pink aprons over their clothes with "Creative Cupcakes" embroidered across the front. "This was taken when we bought the building."

Her heart quickened thinking of that special day. It had been a milestone in their journey to open the cupcake shop and fulfill their dreams.

"It's to remind you that some things in life are more important than money." Bernice patted her hand. "What you girls have here is special, and you were right to turn down the offer from that businessman."

"Thank you, Bernice. I'll put it in the hutch here for everyone to see."

A short while later after Bernice had left, Andi and

Kim's father, William Burke, entered the shop. "Glad to see you didn't quit when you got so busy."

Andi stiffened at the sound of his dry, begrudging tone. Old habits were hard to overcome.

"Of course we didn't quit," she said, forcing a smile. "We aren't quitters."

"Not anymore," her father amended. "I'm glad to see you finally committed to something. You've done a good job here."

It was as close to a compliment as she could get, so she let it go. At least he was trying. Their relationship had been strained since her mother had died, but ever since he saw her determination to make the shop a success, he'd softened.

A few weeks earlier, at Thanksgiving, he'd even thanked the Lord she'd committed to a job and a new marriage. But what would he say if she left the shop and moved away? Would he call her fickle? Would she lose her newly earned respect?

Her mind was so focused on what her father might think of her, she didn't realize Jake had entered the shop.

"Jake, I'm sorry, I didn't see you." She poured him a cup of coffee, and when she slid it toward him, she noticed the telltale crease on his forehead. "Tough day?"

He sank down onto the stool opposite the counter and gave her a half-hearted smile. "Yeah."

"What's wrong?"

He shrugged. "I went to interview several foster parents today, and it didn't go as expected. I'd made appointments, but some of them weren't home."

"Everyone's shopping."

The crease in Jake's forehead deepened. A few of the foster parents I talked to were great, but others . . . didn't seem . . . ." He shook his head. "I feel sorry for those kids trapped in the system, moving from place to place, family to family."

"Rachel's mother has a friend who's a foster parent, and the kids all love her."

"Then her friend is one of the exceptions. There aren't enough good foster parents for all the kids who need homes."

"I see a few foster kids every week," Andi agreed. "Every time I volunteer to pack weekend lunches for the Kids Coalition backpack program or host a free cupcake camp for Mia and Taylor's school friends."

Jake pushed the coffee aside and met her gaze. "I met a boy today. Max. He didn't look like he'd had a decent meal in weeks. I didn't want to pry, but I got the feeling he might be one of the homeless kids living downtown in the 'Shanghai tunnel' under the street. He made me think of our own girls and how lucky we all are to have each other."

Andi frowned. "Max is the name of Mia's imaginary friend. We used to have a dog named Max, and I'm sure that's where she got the name. Today she insisted he was in the back party room, but when I went in, there was nobody there. Maybe she overheard us talking about moving to D.C., got scared, and this is her way of comforting herself. I'm worried about Mia."

"I'm worried about Max," Jake admitted. "What kind of Christmas does he have to look forward to?"

Andi frowned, then said brightly, "I know! We can host a Christmas party for all the foster children in the area. If I ask Mia to help, it might take her mind off her imaginary friend. Local businesses can donate gifts, we can serve cupcakes, and maybe we can even get Mike to dress up as Santa."

"Or *we* could sign up to be foster parents," Jake suggested. "We already have two kids; what's one more?"

"Oh, Jake!" She stared at him and realized he was serious. "I've always dreamed of taking in lots of kids and having a big, happy, home, but—"

"Yes?" Jake asked.

"We have to decide where we're going to live first."

Chapter Five

> Christmas is a day of meaning and traditions, a
> special day spent in the warm circle of family and
> friends.
>
> **—Margaret Thatcher**

UNLIKE GUY, THE tattoo artist, Rachel loved everything
about Christmas: parties, tinsel, mistletoe, lights, music,
shopping, and gifts. She took an ornament out of the box
set on the Creative Cupcakes dining table. "Remember
when we were in the first grade and made these?"

Andi looked at the macaroni angel with gold-painted
hair and white wings, then nodded to her daughter.
"Looks like Mia when she was younger. Now she's growing so fast. She lost the baby fat in her cheeks."

"I guess first grade will do that to you."

Andi sighed. "I miss having her little. She doesn't want me to coddle her as much anymore, especially now that Taylor's living with us, and we're all one family."

"I can't wait to get married and move in with Mike," Rachel said, excitement bubbling up and making her giddy. "Only two more weeks until the wedding."

"Then you and Mike can start your own family," Andi teased.

"Oh, no," Rachel corrected. Had Mike said something to the others? "No babies for me. At least, not right away. It would ruin my figure."

"I guess you're right. Now that I've lost those dreaded ten pounds, the last thing I'd need would be anything to make me gain it all back." Andi held up another ornament. "This is my absolute favorite. My mother made it for me."

Rachel watched Andi put the gray felt bakery mouse clutching the silver spoon on one of the upper branches of the Christmas tree in the corner of the shop. Kim usually set up her art easel and painted in that corner, but they'd convinced her to pack away her paints and brushes until after the holidays.

"Do you think I made a mistake when I planned my wedding for Christmas Eve?" Rachel asked.

"Of course not. Christmas is the season of excitement, glad tidings, and love."

"I had thought the date would be so magical, but now I'm wondering if it will just be interfering with everyone's holiday plans. Several people have told me they can't come."

"What about your cousin? I thought you said she would be here tomorrow."

"Stacey's the one person I wish wouldn't come," Rachel said with a frown.

"Is she bossy?" Andi teased. "Like me?"

"No," Rachel smirked. "More like a bad luck charm. I can't prove it, but every time she's around, disaster strikes. Stacey's quiet, withdrawn, and has no fashion sense. I don't know what I'm going to do with her while she's here. I don't have anything in common with her."

"She could help out in the shop," Andi suggested. "That way we can keep an eye on her for you."

Rachel laughed. "I can't picture Stacey in an apron. Maybe a jail uniform, but not an apron."

"Rachel, drool alert!" Kim warned, from the front counter. "Hot, hunky hero coming through the door."

"I don't drool over anyone but Mike," she called back, but when she saw the man dressed in the Santa suit, she knew he was one and the same.

"Ho, ho, ho!" he greeted her and leaned in close. "Do you have a kiss for Santa?"

She brushed aside the fake white beard. "I prefer my man to be clean shaven, so we can kiss cheek to cheek. I hope you don't intend to wear this to the wedding."

"Don't you want to be Mrs. Claus?" Mike teased.

"Me? In a granny hat, glasses, and an apron?"

"Well, you're already wearing the red apron," he pointed out, and handed her a bag. "Here's the rest of your costume."

Rachel shook her head. "No way."

Andi took her arm. "In exchange for gift donations for the foster kids, I promised some of the local businesses cupcake deliveries from Santa and crew."

Kim leaned over the counter and laughed. "Are you serious?"

"You're going, too," Andi told her. "As an elf. Your first stop is the prenatal class at the Columbia River Health and Fitness club on Olney Avenue. We have an order for a dozen triple-chocolate cupcakes."

Rachel glanced between Andi and Mike. "Prenatal? Isn't that a birthing class?"

Andi smiled. "You're the one who suggested we offer a holiday coupon titled 'Christmas Cupcakes for Stressed-out Dads.'"

Rachel groaned, pulled the white wig and red granny hat over her hair, and followed Mike and Kim out to the Cupcake Mobile. At least she didn't have to wear pointed ears and curly green elf slippers like Kim.

When they arrived at the club, Rachel peered through the door of the prenatal class, hesitant to interrupt. Twelve couples sat on the floor, each with a pillow and a mat. It looked like the instructor was teaching the women different ways to stretch and breathe. The men were there to support and lift, but many had clueless expressions on their faces as if they had no idea what to do.

"See what we have to look forward to?" Mike murmured against her ear.

Rachel stared at all the fat stomachs. "Is that how you want me to look? Like a big, round snowball with only my head, arms, and feet sticking out?"

"Chasing after our children would whip your figure back into shape," he said, giving her waist a quick squeeze.

"Yeah, dragging around a brood of drooling, dependent kids in diapers seems like the perfect workout," she drawled.

The instructor must have either seen them by the door or heard them whispering, because she stopped the exercise and looked right at them. "Can I help you?"

Rachel stepped forward with the delivery box. "Which dad gets the cupcakes?"

None of the men acknowledged her, but a woman with a *very* large stomach struggled to her feet and pointed to the man beside her. "They belong to him."

"I didn't order any," he protested.

The pregnant woman who stood, wobbled forward and took the box from Rachel's hands. "I called."

The man Rachel assumed was the woman's husband asked, "You did?"

"I have this coupon titled 'Christmas Cupcakes for Stressed-out Dads,'" the woman explained. "And you look really stressed."

As the woman took a series of deep breaths, Rachel thought she was the one who looked stressed.

Her husband looked around the room, embarrassment coloring his cheeks. "I'm fine."

The woman stumbled, tucked the bakery box against her chest with one arm, and clutched Rachel's arm for support with her other. "Believe me, you are stressed," she told her husband. "Now, come get the cupcakes so you can share them with me."

Rachel winced from the tight grip the woman had on her arm and looked to Mike for help.

"Here, let me take the box for you," Mike offered.

"No!" the woman shouted and bared her teeth in a near snarl. "I need these cupcakes, and I need them now!"

Her husband gasped. "Dolores, what's gotten into you?"

The other couples started closing in on her as Dolores opened the box, and the aroma of freshly baked chocolate cupcakes with triple-chocolate creamy frosting filled the air.

"I could use a cupcake," another woman said. "I've been having a craving for cupcakes all morning."

"So have I," said another.

"Back off!" Dolores warned. "They're all mine!"

Another worried husband asked, "Do you have any more?"

"Yes," Mike said, "out in the truck."

"You better hurry," the instructor told him. "I've seen this happen before, and believe me—it can get ugly."

When Rachel, Mike, and Kim returned, each carrying four boxes of cupcakes, Dolores was on the floor in obvious pain, her cupcakes abandoned.

"She's going into labor," the instructor announced and snapped her cell phone shut. "I called the hospital, but the ambulance can't get through for another twenty minutes. There's been an accident, and some of the roads have been blocked off."

"He drove me here in a Volkswagen Beetle," Dolores said, glaring at her husband between puffs of breath. "I can't lie down in a Beetle! He wanted that stupid car, not me."

"The ambulance will be here in just a few more minutes," her husband said, patting her arm.

"I don't have another few minutes!" Dolores screeched. "I've been having contractions all day but didn't want to say anything until the cupcakes arrived. I thought it was just more false labor like I've been having all week . . . but *this . . . is . . . real.*"

Another contraction must have started for she grimaced, drew in a breath, and let it back out between clenched teeth in a series of short huffs and hisses.

"We can take her in the Cupcake Mobile," Mike said and met Rachel's gaze.

Take Dolores to the hospital? Hey, why not? At least the woman had helped sell a truck full of cupcakes. Rachel took off her Mrs. Claus granny glasses and put them in the pocket of her apron. "Kim, you stay here and serve cupcakes, and we'll come back for you."

Kim nodded. "This is one trip I'd rather not take."

AFTER TEN MINUTES getting Dolores into the back of the Cupcake Mobile and another fifteen minutes on the road, Rachel had to agree with Kim. Dolores was sweating like she'd come out of an oven and snapping at her husband ten times worse than William Burke snapped at his daughter, Andi.

"I see the head!" Dolores's husband shouted.

"What?" Rachel looked into the back of the Cupcake Mobile. "This is no place to give birth!"

"The Nativity didn't take place in the most ideal conditions either," Mike reminded her. "And still a miracle was born."

The next few minutes whirled past in a fast and furious blur. Mike pulled over, and Rachel helped him push aside boxes in the back of the truck to give Dolores more room. A police car pulled up behind them and two uniformed officers, whom Dolores's husband had conversed with on the phone, prepared to assist with the birth. The woman screamed, and Rachel thought she screamed with her.

Then there was another person in the Cupcake Mobile, and when ready, Rachel used her red apron to wrap the newborn and hand him to his mother. Dolores smiled, her husband smiled, and Rachel found that despite the horrific panic she'd felt moments before, she was now smiling, too.

She'd never witnessed a baby's first cry or seen such tiny fingers and toes. Even after the first few moments of birth she thought the child had his father's mouth and his mother's eyes. Certainly, he had their love.

Dolores appeared a tired but transformed woman. Her husband, whom Rachel thought to be one of the most forgiving people in the world, held her close as if she'd never uttered an unkind word against him. Together, they held their baby and looked like the happiest family on the planet.

Rachel looked at Mike, and he put his arm around her as they shared in this family's special moment.

"What do you think now?" Mike asked, his eyes lit with mischief. "Still against motherhood?"

"No," Rachel conceded. "Someday ... when we're ready, a family of our own might be ... nice."

And when that day came, she'd want to be right here in Astoria, not down in Hollywood amid glitzy lights and movie star billboards. Mike had mentioned moving, but she couldn't imagine ever bringing a child into the world without her mother and best friends by their side.

No, Astoria is where she'd stay because, together, they'd always be okay.

KIM DIDN'T THINK she'd ever forget the expression on Rachel's face when she came back to the Columbia River Health and Fitness club and announced, "It's a boy!"

Her friend's exuberance stayed with her as she and Nathaniel accompanied Andi, Jake, and their girls sledding the next day.

Seven inches of snow had blanketed the hillsides of Astoria overnight, closing the schools. Eighth Street, one of the steepest streets in the whole country, with its wavy, forty-five-degree angle, had also been closed and transformed into a premier sledding hill for local residents.

As a light flurry of snow continued to swirl down, Kim tightened the scarf around her neck and pulled the wool hood of her coat up over her head.

"Bye, Kim!" Mia yelled. She waved as she and Andi doubled up on a saucer sled and slid down the snowpack.

Kim sat down on her elongated two-man sled and called, "Taylor, are you sure you don't want to come with me?"

Taylor rolled a large ball of snow with her father and shook her head. "We're building a snowman."

"I'll go with you." Nathaniel scooted behind her on the sled and wrapped his arms around her. "Ready?"

Kim tucked her boots into the front of the sled and nodded. "I haven't been sledding in years."

The sled dipped, flattened out over the next cross street, dipped again, gained speed, and sent them tumbling off into a snow bank.

Nathaniel laughed. "Want to go again?"

"Oh, yes!" Kim smiled, wishing she could preserve this moment forever. She and Nathaniel—together—not just for the present, but for all time.

As they trudged back up the hill, she waved a mittened hand toward the dozens of children laughing and playing all around them. "Do you ever picture yourself having kids someday?"

Nathaniel's blue eyes sparkled as he turned and gave her a sideways grin. "*Ja*, of course."

"But . . . you can't travel much when you have kids."

"Sure you can. Just strap them on your back and take them with you. Fredrik, Linnea, and I never tied my mother down. We'd each been to seventeen countries before the age of five."

"Are you serious?" Kim studied his face and found he was. "Your mom must have been a strong woman."

"She just loved us too much to leave us behind."

Nathaniel took her hand and pulled her up a steep stretch of the slippery slope. "Fredrik bought tickets to fly to Göteborg for Christmas. I think he wants to show off his new wife to the folks back home who couldn't come over for the wedding."

"Do you picture yourself getting married someday?" She held her breath, unable to bring herself to look at him.

"*Ja,* I suppose it would be hard to have a kid without being married," he teased.

"Some people do," she protested.

"I'm not 'some people,' Kimberly. Before I have kids, I will marry." He grinned. "If the woman I choose accepts me."

"First you'd have to propose." There! She'd said it. *Oh, my gosh!* She'd actually said it out loud.

"*Ja,*" he said, his voice warm. "I suppose you're right."

She sneaked a peek at his face. He was smiling, grinning from ear to ear, but wasn't getting down on one knee.

"I have a proposal for you," he said, when they crested the top, sled in hand.

Kim could hardly breathe. "Yes?"

"What if we take a trip to the Flavel House this evening? I hear they're serving Christmas tea with plum pudding."

"Plum pudding?" she demanded. After coming so close to actually talking about a possible future together, he was offering her plum pudding?

"Or we could go to the Liberty Theater to see *The Nutcracker.*"

"*The Nutcracker,*" she repeated, her throat dry.

Then her heart quickened. What if he proposed to her this evening? Of course! He probably already had the whole thing planned out. Instead of a haphazard proposal on a sled hill, he would propose tonight when they were dressed nice and out on a real date. A romantic date.

She flung her arms around his neck and gave him a quick kiss. "Plum pudding at the Flavel House sounds perfect."

Chapter Six

Sing hey! Sing hey!
For Christmas Day;
Twine mistletoe and holly.
For a friendship glows,
In winter snows,
And so let's all be jolly!

—Author Unknown

MAX SCOOPED UP a handful of snow, packed it into a ball, threw it in the air, then hit it with his drumstick.

Not a good idea. The cold, powdery remains flew into his face. Then it melted against his skin and ran down his bare neck. He turned up the collar of his flannel shirt so it wouldn't happen again.

As he packed his next snowball, he looked toward Mia

and her family. He'd been watching them for an hour—laughing, playing, sledding. Maybe when his mother came back they'd go sledding and have good times—like *them*. Like a real family should.

He thought about going over and saying "hey" to Jake, but . . . the guy was too busy tossing snowballs back and forth with Mia's mom. Maybe some other time.

He sliced another snowball with his drumstick, then turned his head toward the raised voice of a mean, fat kid from his class at school.

The boy, Toby Pittenger, better known as Toby the Pit Bull, was arguing with some little kid over a sled. Max edged closer to listen in.

"You're in the way!" Toby shouted. "Get off the hill, or I'll break your sled in two."

"That's my sled," a small voice whined. "Give it back."

Toby turned sideways, and Max sucked in his breath when he saw the kid being bullied was Mia.

"Give her back her sled," Max said, closing the distance between them.

"Who are you, the kid's brother or something?"

Max stuck out his chin. "That sled isn't yours. Give it back. *Now.*"

"Like I would listen to you."

Max growled and raised his drumstick, ready to strike.

"I was just foolin' around," Toby said, throwing the saucer sled at Mia's feet. "Since when do *you* care, anyway?"

Max didn't lower his arm until Toby was a safe distance. Then he took Mia's hand and pulled her back up on her feet.

"Thanks, Max."

"No problem." He held the sled steady while Mia climbed on. "No one should treat you like that. No one. If that kid bothers you again, I want to hear about it."

"Okay, Max," she said, a smile back on her face. "Do you want to sled with me?"

"Maybe later." He glanced over at Jake, who caught sight of him and waved. "There's someone I need to talk to."

Jake might be the first person he'd met who could help. He must have connections—know people—from working at the *Astoria Sun*. Maybe he could write up an ad to find his mom, let her know he still waited for her, let her know he'd been placed in foster care.

And if Jake couldn't help, he'd find her himself, because he was through putting up with the Tobys of this world. Just like he was through with bad foster parents who took the money meant to supply him with food and clothes and used it to buy lottery tickets. Once he found his mom, everything would be great. He'd never be in foster care ever again.

Later that night, Max returned from a scavenger trek around town to find Jake on his doorstep, speaking with Garth Gilmore, his current foster care provider. No way! What was he doing here? When he talked with Jake earlier, he didn't tell him his last name or where he lived.

He dove behind the bushes next to the front steps before anyone could see him.

"My wife isn't here right now," Garth said cheerfully. "She must have run to the store to buy some groceries."

Yeah, right, Max thought. Paula had moved out a month before, and their refrigerator had remained bare ever since.

"So you and your wife live together?" Jake asked. "You aren't getting a divorce?"

"No, no divorce. Did Max tell you that?" Garth laughed as if amused. "Max Holloway is very disturbed. We treat Max like gold, but he lies, steals, cheats. Seems like we're always pulling him out of some kind of trouble."

Max clenched his drumstick, wishing he could beat it on something. After this, Jake would never treat him like a friend, never invite him to jam with him at the music store, never buy him anything else to eat.

"Maybe I can help," Jake told Garth. "I'm part-owner of Creative Cupcakes, and my wife is gathering donated gifts from local businesses to distribute to foster kids this weekend. Can I put Max's name on the list?"

"Go ahead," Garth said, "and when you publish your article about me, remember to spell my last name with an *e* on the end. Oh, and make sure you include my quote about how hard we work as foster parents and how we only want what's best for the child."

"I will," Jake promised and snapped his notepad shut.

The sound made Max jump, and Jake turned his head. He saw him. But to his surprise, Jake didn't rat him out. Instead, he gave a final nod to Garth, got in his shiny blue Mazda Miata, and drove away.

Max slumped against the wall of the house and

squeezed his eyes shut. Jake wouldn't come back. He had his news story, his fancy car, his merry little family . . . and a holly-jolly cupcake shop decked out for Christmas with lights, bows, tinsel, cranberries, and popcorn strings.

What would he want with *him*?

SATURDAY AFTERNOON ANDI stacked the brightly colored wrapped packages in the back party room for Mike to load into the Cupcake Mobile and argued with the next-door neighbor.

"Guy," she pleaded. "I'm not asking to pull your other tooth out. All I want is a donation for the foster kids."

The tattoo artist grinned in response, revealing his missing left canine. "Pulling a tooth would be easier for me than turning into Santa. At least I'd have a matched pair."

"Do you want to be naughty or nice?" she demanded. "How would you feel if you were a kid and didn't get a gift on Christmas?"

Guy scowled. "There's been many times when I didn't."

"So you *do* know how it feels," Andi said, her hands on her hips. "The Pig 'N' Pancake, Maritime Museum, Coastguard, the Captain's Port, and Safeway grocery have all donated."

"So what do you need me to give up my hard-earned money for?" he protested.

Rachel brought another gift in to add to the pile. "A kiss under the mistletoe might soften him up."

"I'm too old for mistletoe," Guy hissed.

Rachel's mom, Sarah, also carried in a gift. "Guess what, Andi? I got a loan to open a bridal shop."

"Congratulations!" Andi said. "You've done a wonderful job sewing all our dresses."

The glow on Sarah's face lit her eyes. "Watching you three girls go after your dream to open a cupcake shop inspired me to go after my own dream."

Andi thought of Jake's job offer in Washington and how badly he wanted it. "Yes," she said and swallowed hard. "Everyone should have the opportunity to pursue a dream."

"People can't just pursue their dreams," Rachel amended. "They need to *fight* for them. And Astoria is known as the 'home of the fighting fishermen.'"

"But you're not fishermen; you're cupcake shop owners," Guy reminded her.

Rachel shrugged. "Does it matter?"

"You have inspired me, too, Guy," Sarah told him. "I admire the way you left the space here in the back room and expanded your business in the building next door."

Guy grinned. "You were inspired by *me*?"

"I was just telling Guy how he should be inspired to donate gifts for the foster children," Andi said, giving Sarah a wink.

"Oh, that's a wonderful idea," Sarah agreed. "You *will* donate a few gifts, won't you, Guy?"

Guy looked at Sarah, and his grin turned into a full-fledged smile. "Okay, I'll do it for the kids."

When Andi returned to the front of the shop, Rachel

introduced her cousin. "This is Stacey McIntyre from Coeur d'Alene, Idaho."

"Nice to meet you," Andi said, shaking her hand. "Rachel tells me you're willing to work while you're here for the wedding."

The young woman wore one red sock and one green. Andi tried not to stare at her feet, but couldn't help herself—and Stacey noticed.

"When I woke up this morning, I couldn't find a match," Stacey explained.

"That's okay," Andi assured her. "Your socks are a perfect match for our red aprons and the green bandanas we wear over our hair."

Rachel opened the Cupcake Diary and read off their latest plans. "Today we started our 'Twelve Days of Christmas' theme. We're serving pear cupcakes topped with a tiny partridge made of multicolored piped icing. Tomorrow we serve twin turtle doves on our eggnog-flavored cupcakes. On the third day—"

"Three French hens?" Stacey asked with a giggle.

"You got it," Andi said, nodding. "On the fourth day we serve up cupcakes with plastic bird whistles for 'four calling birds,' and on the fifth day we decorate the cupcakes with five golden rings."

"Five!" Kim called out. "I can't even get one!"

Andi looked across the room to the table where her sister was creating a Santa sleigh and reindeer out of cupcakes. She'd used red string licorice for the reins, pretzels for antlers, and a red gumdrop for Rudolph's nose.

"I didn't know you wanted Nathaniel to propose," she said, glancing at Rachel to see if she knew.

Rachel shook her head, her mouth open in surprise.

"I thought for sure he'd propose when he took me to the Flavel House two nights ago for plum pudding," Kim said, poking another reindeer cupcake with a chocolate chip nose. "You know I did research on Swedish traditions, and when someone finds an almond in a special rice porridge, it's supposed to mean they'll get married in the coming year. I figured plum pudding was kind of like rice porridge, but did I get an almond? No! No almond. No proposal. *Nothing.*"

Andi gasped at her sister's unaccustomed show of emotion. "Do you want me to give him a hint?"

Kim shook her head. "Don't you dare!"

Andi would have liked to learn more about this new development, but the phone rang, and she was the closest one to answer it. "Hello, Creative Cupcakes."

She hoped the caller on the other end might be Jake, but it was that dreaded businessman Preston Pennyworth again.

"I'm willing to make you a new offer," he informed her. "I'll tack on another two hundred and fifty thousand."

"One point four five million bucks?" Andi glanced at the wood hutch in the dining area where they had placed all the cupcake-shaped gifts their loyal customers had brought in to give to them: candles, cards, piggy banks, picture frames, salt-and-pepper shakers, plates, bowls, and candy. She let out a low whistle. "That's a lot of money. I'll have to think about it."

"When will you know?" he persisted.

"Well, I'll have to talk it over with my partners."

"Can you do it tonight?"

She looked around the shop, filled with customers coming in and out, employees running back and forth, the gifts for the foster kids stacked and ready to go. "No, I'm busy."

"Then when can I expect an answer?"

Mia ran past her with a stocking that had glitter flying off onto the floor.

Andi placed her hand over the phone's mouthpiece. "Mia, look what you're doing!"

Mia held up the stocking, and Andi read the name she'd written on it with glue and gold glitter. *Max.*

"You made a stocking for your imaginary friend?" Andi asked, shaking her head.

"He's *real*, Mom!" Mia argued.

"Andi, did you hear what I said?"

Mr. Pennyworth's voice drew her attention back to the phone. "Yes, I heard you."

"I need an answer within the next three days. I want to give Creative Cupcakes to my daughter for Christmas."

Give Creative Cupcakes away as a Christmas gift? The company she'd worked her sweet bum off to make a success? This was *her* dream, *her* inspiration, and she wasn't about to just let it go to the likes of him.

"You know what? I don't have to wait another minute. You want an answer? The answer is *no*."

As she hung up the phone, Rachel asked, "Who was that?"

Guilt shot through Andi as she realized she'd made another rash decision without consulting her lifelong pals. But her answer to the guy would have been the same.

"Phone solicitor," she replied.

Rachel scowled. "They're always asking for money around the holidays."

"Just like you're asking for donated gifts?" Ian Lockwell teased, carrying an armload of presents. "These were donated by our division for the foster kids. Where do you want them?"

Andi pointed to the party room. "Mike's loading up the Cupcake Mobile tonight so we can deliver the gifts first thing in the morning."

"Hope you lock the truck up tight," Ian warned. "There's always a lot of theft this time of year."

"Don't worry," Andi said, giving him a big smile. "We've got the best locks on our truck and our shop doors, we now have an indoor *and* an outdoor security camera, and I've set up a neighborhood watch. I'm not going to let anyone steal away our Christmas!"

ANDI ROSE AT the crack of dawn and rushed to the grocery store for some extra food coloring, candy canes, sugar sprinkles, and cinnamon red-hots. Next, she rushed to the post office to mail her Christmas cards, only to remember it was Sunday, and the post office wasn't open. Then she rushed to the variety shop on the corner to pick up a few last-minute gifts to add to the ones in the Cupcake Mobile.

She was beginning to see why Guy thought Christmas was the season of stress with all the shopping, buying, wrapping, decorating, baking, not enough time in the day, rush, rush, rush. To add to the craziness, someone backed into her in the parking lot and dented her car. *How cliché.*

She and the other driver exchanged phone numbers and insurance information, but the experience took her out of her "Joy to the World" mood.

"Merry Christmas!" Andi muttered under her breath, as her car's assailant drove away.

Beside her, Mia put her hands together in a *clap—clap, clap, clap—clap* rhythm and chanted, "Who let the Grinch out? Who! Who!"

Andi recognized the tune, although the words had been changed. "Are you implying I sound like a Grinch?"

Mia nodded, and Andi resolved to change her attitude. If she and Jake decided to move, she didn't want to remember this Christmas in a negative way. No, she wanted to hear the "resounding joy" as the children opened their packages and see the look of wonder on their angelic faces.

However, "angelic" would not be the word she'd use to describe the expressions of Mike, Rachel, Stacey, Jake, and Kim when she drove up to the Cupcake Mobile. They were all there.

But the gifts were not.

Chapter Seven

Christmas is a time when you get homesick—
even when you're home.

—Carol Nelson

"How could the gifts be stolen?" Andi demanded, circling the truck. "How did they break in?"

"Through the passenger side window," Mike pointed. "Whoever did this smashed the glass to smithereens."

Rachel handed her a piece of paper. "Look what he left."

"*Compliments of the Grinch,*" Andi read. She spun around and glanced at the big, green, hairy Grinch cartoon painted on the front of their shop window. "He must have got the 'Grinch' idea from us! Kim, why didn't you wash that off?"

"People like it, and besides, whoever vandalized the shop and stole the gifts is probably the same person."

"A person who thinks he's funny," Rachel said with a frown and glanced at Stacey.

Stacey's eyes widened at the silent accusation, but she didn't say a word. Instead, she crossed her arms over her chest and bit her lip.

"Did the security camera pick anything up?" Andi asked.

Mike shook his head. "The camera we installed outside the shop faces the front of the building, not the street."

"What about Guy?" Andi looked at each of their faces. "Did you ask if he saw anything? Or if any of the other local business owners noticed anything odd?"

"No," Kim told her. "No one saw anything."

The full impact of the situation hit Andi with brute force, and she suddenly felt sick. "What are we going to do? I can't let all those kids down."

Jake closed the open doors on the back of the Cupcake Mobile. "We can start collecting new presents."

"Ask everyone to donate again? How can I guarantee they'll be delivered?" Andi thought of all those poor foster kids without a gift on Christmas day, and she ran and threw up in the bushes.

This was all her fault. She'd been too confident when telling Ian that no thief would be able to steal from them. Why, anyone who had overheard her would have considered it an open invitation.

I'm not going to let anyone steal away our Christmas!

Mia was right. All this holiday craziness was turning *her* into a Grinch. But only if she let it.

She drew in a deep breath, straightened, and returned to the group. "Somehow we've got to get gifts to the foster kids by Christmas."

Mia looked up at her with those big blue eyes and asked, "There's still hope?"

Andi wiped a stray tear away, gave into a quick smile, and nodded. "Yes. There's always hope. Meantime, we'll put out a reward—a dozen peppermint hot chocolate cupcakes to whoever helps us catch the Grinch."

MONDAY MORNING, RACHEL arranged for their employees to watch over the shop while she, Andi, and Kim tried on dresses for the final fitting.

"We tried them on last week, and they were fine, Mom," Rachel said with a smile. "But you know how I like looking at myself in the mirror."

" 'Cinderella' is conceited," Kim teased.

Rachel laughed. "Yeah, but you know it's true. Just wait until you get married someday."

Kim pressed her lips together. "Yeah, can't wait."

Rachel slid the mass of white satin and lace over her head, but when she looked in the mirror, her eyes were drawn to something dark smudged on the skirt of her dress. She sucked in her breath. "What's that?"

"What?" Sarah asked with a frown.

"I *do* look like Cinderella, and not in a good way! What is that on my gown?"

Andi bent down to take a peek, and when she rose, her face had paled, and her eyes warned of trouble. "Rachel—"

"Andi, what is it?"

"Cranberry walnut cupcake with creamy dark fudge."

Rachel gasped as she picked up the material and drew it closer. "How did cupcake get on my gown?"

"It's on my gown, too," Andi told her, "and Kim's."

"This is a disaster!" Rachel shouted. "The most important day of my life, and our dresses are soiled by cupcakes?"

She shot a look at her mother. "It must be Stacey. Ever since she arrived, there's been trouble. First the gifts were stolen out of the truck, now *this*."

"You can't blame your cousin," Sarah scolded. "It could have been your grandfather. You know how he loves cupcakes."

"And Stacey wasn't here when the cupcake shop was vandalized," Kim reminded her.

"This could still be her doing," Rachel protested.

Sarah threw her hands up in the air. "It was your idea to have a party here this weekend to try to raise money to buy new gifts for the foster kids. You know we have a tiny house. You should have had the party at the cupcake shop."

"It was a spur-of-the-moment event, and you shouldn't have had the wedding gowns hanging on the rack in the hallway."

"Are you blaming *me* for this?"

Rachel burst into tears and threw her arms around

her mother's neck. "No, I'm so sorry, Mom. I didn't mean it. But—look at me! The wedding is next week. Can we clean the dresses in time?"

Sarah looked as if she were trying not to cry. "I'll do my best. I just hope it doesn't stain."

KIM TOOK HER paints and brushes up the hill to Astor Elementary, where Mia and Taylor went to school. The cartoon murals on the side of the building had been originally painted by local artists for the filming of the movie *Kindergarten Cop* starring Arnold Schwarzenegger. Today, she'd promised the woman in charge of its upkeep that she'd refresh the paint before more snow moved into the area.

When she rounded the corner, she discovered a boy of about eleven or twelve on a ladder painting over the brown spots on the bright, yellow giraffe.

"Looks good," Kim said, admiring his work. "You must be Max Holloway."

The boy turned his head to look at her and nodded.

"I'm Kimberly Burke. I was recruited to help you—although I was told you're one of the best painters in the sixth grade." She watched his brushstrokes and frowned, the front window of Creative Cupcakes flitting through her mind. "Do you know how to paint the Grinch?"

"I don't paint much," the boy said, dabbing paint on another brown dot. "I like drawing better."

"Charcoal, pen, or pencil?"

"Pencil."

Kim pointed to the sketchbook sticking out of the black backpack by his feet. "Can I see?"

Max climbed down the ladder, set down his brush, and wiped his hands on a white cloth. "They aren't great."

Kim took the sketchbook he handed her and flipped through the pages. The first image was of a pilot boat used by the Coast Guard to help navigate ships through the Columbia River.

"These are wonderful," she said, looking at the next drawing of a wooden dock covered with sea lions. "You've really captured the fine details."

She turned to the next page. There was a sketch of a woman about her age, in her mid to late twenties. The woman's expression was sorrowful, yet it held a hint of hope. "Who's this?"

Max looked away. "My mother."

"Has she seen this?"

"No."

"You should show her," Kim encouraged. "I think she'd like to see this, Max."

"She left." He turned back around and met her gaze. "She promised to come back for Christmas, but she never did."

Kim hesitated. "And your father?"

"In jail. He gave up his rights to me a long time ago."

"I'm sorry, Max." She didn't know what else to say. "My mother died in a plane crash a long time ago. I do have a father, but . . . we're not very close."

"Were you in foster care?"

"What? Me?" Kim laughed, but then sobered when

she saw his expression. "No. No, I wasn't. Are you in foster care, Max?"

He shrugged and reached out for the sketchbook but not before she turned the page and saw the drawing of Creative Cupcakes.

"You drew a picture of my shop." She glanced up and caught the startled look in his eyes. *Was* he the boy who painted a Grinch on their storefront window?

"My mother used to work there," he said, taking back his sketches. "Before the place was a cupcake shop, it used to be called—"

"Zeke's Tavern," Kim finished. A closer look revealed his sketch was of the building before they'd added their frilly pink-and-white curtains and changed the name on the sign.

"I used to play there while she worked," Max said softly. "Sometimes it still feels like . . . home."

Kim stared at him, trying to imagine what his life must have been like up to this point, and something inside her clicked into place, like an answer to an unspoken question.

"I know the feeling, Max," she said, opening a can of paint. "Everyone needs a home."

MAX LEANED AGAINST the side of the building, next to the back party room door, waiting for Mia to come back. She'd already given him a coat, actually—it was a black magician's cape—which she said might help him disappear if he really wanted to. It didn't work, but at least it kept him warm. And in couple of minutes she'd return with a cupcake.

The side door opened, and Mia held out a white candy bird on top of whipped blue frosting. "Do you know the song about the twelve days of Christmas? Today is seven swans a swimming."

"Awesome." The smell of the sweet creamy icing was nothing compared to the homemade taste of the vanilla cake when he popped it into his mouth. "Must be great owning your own cupcake shop."

Mia scrunched up her nose. "They won't let me use the mixer or the oven. So I asked Santa for my own Easy-Bake Oven for Christmas."

Max finished off the cupcake and threw the wrapper in the garbage can beside him on the street. "I don't believe there is a Santa Claus."

"Yes, there is," Mia argued.

"I never get presents."

"Did you tell him you moved? Maybe he doesn't know where you live."

"Believe me, Santa wouldn't want to come to *my* house."

Mia frowned. "Why not?"

Max shook his head. She was just a little girl. What did *she* know? "Well, for one thing, we don't have cookies waiting for him; there's no tree, no stocking—"

"I made you a stocking," Mia said, her eyes wide. "I hung it on the wall of the shop next to mine. Santa Claus has to give you a present this year."

"All I want is for my mom to come back." He dug in his

pocket and took out the postcard he'd kept for the last six years. "When she left, she handed me this picture of Hawaii. She told me to stay here, and she'd be back before Christmas. Then she'd take me there. But she never came back."

"Is she in Hawaii?"

Max looked at the white sand beach and palm trees on the front of the postcard. "I don't know."

"My dad left and never came back." Mia frowned again. "That made my mom cry. Then we met Jake and Taylor, and Taylor didn't have a mom. Now my mom is her mom, and her dad is my dad, and we are a new family. Do you want a new family, Max?"

Before he could answer, voices came from inside the party room behind her.

"Oh, no," Mia whispered. "Here they come. I have to go, Max. Bye!"

Mia ran from the door but left it open a crack. Max peered inside, careful not to let anyone see him. Two people entered the room, Jake and Mia's mom.

"I spoke with his social worker," Jake said, "and she confirmed that the Gilmores have filed for divorce. Mrs. Gilmore isn't even living there, and Mr. Gilmore said she did. He lied right to my face."

"Sounds like he just wanted his name in the paper," Mia's mother replied.

"Max was there," Jake said, his voice raw, "hiding in the bushes, listening to that guy paint him as some kind of monster. I feel sorry for him, Andi. Earlier that same day, Max came up to me on the sled hill and asked if I could help find his mom—but that's not happening."

Mia's mother dipped her head to catch Jake's eye. She looked concerned. "Why not?"

Jake let out a grunt. "Max said his mother promised to come back before Christmas. He thinks she never returned. But she did."

"And?"

"I found out she signed away her parental rights just like his drunken drifter of a father did a few years before."

No! Max sucked in his breath. It couldn't be true. Jake was lying, just like his foster father had lied. They were all a bunch of liars.

Suddenly, his eyes burned, and he pulled himself away from the door. In fact, he was so filled with heat he didn't even need the stupid cape Mia had given him. Ripping it off, he threw it to the ground and stomped on it again and again.

"What happens now?" Andi's mother asked, her voice faint.

Max paused in his cape stomping to listen—even though Jake was a no-good-dirty-stinking liar.

"Right after Christmas he's being placed with another family, but he'll be in foster care until he's eighteen."

Max could hardly breathe, probably because of all the energy he'd used to stomp on the cape. His heart pounded in his chest, and his stomach squeezed tight.

He looked at the postcard still in his hand. Why had he kept this ratty thing for so long? There wasn't even any handwriting on the back. After tearing Hawaii in two, he lifted the lid of the garbage can and threw the pieces in with the remains of his finished cupcake.

"Hey!" someone shouted. "What are you doing here?"

Not just someone, but Garth Gilmore.

A wave of weakness flooded over Max, making him dizzy. That's probably what made it so easy for Garth to grab him by the shirt collar and haul him away.

Chapter Eight

> The best of all gifts around any Christmas tree:
> the presence of a happy family all wrapped up in
> each other.
>
> **—Burton Hillis**

"STOLEN *AGAIN*?" ANDI demanded. "How is that possible?"

She looked around the vacant shop, trying to quell the uneasiness in her stomach. The day before, Creative Cupcakes could have been mistaken for Santa's workshop with all of the colorful new gifts, toys, candies, and little "elf" kids running around. Today, there was nothing left to suggest Christmas was only two days away—no tree, no red stockings, no mistletoe. Worse, the handmade gray bakery mouse ornament her mother had made her so many years ago had also been taken.

As the room spun, she gripped the counter. Her mother's ornament was irreplaceable, one of a kind. Something she'd never get back.

"There's no sign of breaking and entering," Ian Lockwell informed her. "The thief must have had a key to come into the shop and then lock the door on his way out, unless he dropped down from the roof. But since you don't have a chimney, I think we can rule that out."

"How would this thief get a key?" Rachel asked. "From one of our employees?"

Kim shook her head. "Eric, Heather, and Theresa deny losing or giving their key to anyone."

"And if it wasn't any of us," Andi said, trying to think, "or the guys . . . that means somehow someone got a key to this shop without us knowing about it, or he found a way to magically appear inside."

Rachel pursed her lips. "Should we ask Mike for ideas? He knows about magic tricks."

"Yes," Kim agreed. "But why would he take our tree?"

Andi frowned. "It's as if the culprit shanghaied the tree and all the new gifts I'd collected for the foster children. Except our shop doesn't have a trapdoor or a hatch leading out of the building like the Captain's Port."

"He must have used the side door of the back party room," Ian explained, "because the interior security camera showed he didn't use the front door. Whoever did this came up to the camera from the inside and smashed a cupcake into the lens before it could get a clear shot of him."

Andi pointed to the pages of the Cupcake Diary

spread out on the counter next to the glass display case and looked at Rachel and Kim. "Did you leave this open?"

Both shook their heads and drew closer.

Rachel's eyes widened as she read, *"Got Grinch?"*

"This person isn't just being funny," Kim said, pointing to the green lettering. "He wants to be known."

Rachel waved her hand toward the coatrack. "Can you believe it? The Grinch even stole Mike's red Santa suit."

"He really *is* a Grinch!" Kim said with a scowl.

"I guess you don't have to worry about Mike wearing the Santa suit at your wedding," Andi said, glancing at Rachel.

She'd meant the comment as a joke, but the crack in her voice ruined the humor. All she could think about was that she'd failed again, failed to gather the gifts she'd promised those poor foster care children.

Later that day, Andi agreed when Jake suggested they take the girls to the Port of Ilwaco Christmas celebration. Jake needed to write an article on the event, and he said it might help take her mind off the Grinch and all his cold-hearted thievery.

Ilwaco, Washington, was just a short ride over Oregon's Astoria-Megler Bridge, and many of Astoria's locals made the trip to see "the World's Tallest Crab Pot Christmas Tree," "the World's Shortest Fireworks Display," and the renowned Lighted Boat Parade.

Mia and Taylor, excited to be off from school for two whole weeks of winter break, ran ahead as she and Jake strolled through the Christmas Market featuring Pacific Northwest arts and crafts vendors. Caroling and the lively, uplifting music of the jazz band filled the frosty night air.

Jake stopped at a food booth and bought them each a slice of pizza. "Reminds me of the pizzeria my family owned when I was growing up. Can you smell the fresh oregano and garlic?"

Andi could smell it, all right. "I can taste it, too. You won't want to kiss me after this."

Jake grinned. "Of course I will. I was raised around people with pizza breath. You know the East Coast is famous for its pizza. My grandmother came from Italy and helped my father start his first pizza store in New York. Then Dad decided to move to Lake Tahoe, and our family started a second store there."

Andi's gaze traveled past him to a tent vendor selling ornaments. "You know, some of those look familiar. I'll be right back."

She browsed the Christmas ornaments decorating the six mini tabletop trees lining the fold-out table and pointed to a painted glass ball with a reindeer.

"Where did you get this?" she asked the seller.

The woman pointed to another vendor three tents down who sold the same generic ornaments. "Would you like to buy?"

"No, thank you," Andi said and returned to Jake and the girls.

"A change of scenery might be good for you," Jake said, taking her arm. "Have you thought more about—"

"Jake! The tree lighting is about to start." She waved to the girls to throw their pizza-stained napkins in the trash and taking their hands, led them toward the gathering crowd.

Dozens upon dozens of stainless steel boxed-wire crab pots had been stacked one on top of the other, forming the shape of a giant tree. A golden star lit the top, and the rest of the "tree" was decorated with multicolored lights and hundreds of fishing lures.

"Looks like it's at least twenty-five feet tall," Jake said and scribbled a few lines in his notebook. "Almost as big as the Capitol Christmas tree in Washington, D.C."

Andi pointed past the tree to another vendor. "Do you see the bag of presents that guy is holding?"

"The man by the beach offering Pirate Santa Photos?" Jake shot her a look of sympathy. "Andi, the guy's legit. Those aren't the gifts stolen from our shop."

"I'm sorry. I keep picturing the foster children having a blue Christmas like in that old TV special, *The Year without a Santa Claus.*"

The Lighted Boat Parade immediately followed. Floating vessels of all shapes and sizes, from dinghies to crabbers, sailed past in single file through the marina. They went out to Cape Disappointment and back, giving people plenty of time to judge which boat's lighted mast, garlands, and other festive holiday decor they liked best.

While the red, blue, yellow, and green lights reflected in the dark nighttime water were some of the prettiest images she'd ever seen, Andi's gaze strayed back toward the vendors, especially to one man selling gifts and ornaments out of the back of an open truck.

Excusing herself, she left Jake with the girls and made

her way toward him. He even had some macaroni angels, similar to the ones she and Rachel had made when they were younger, except with different decorative detail.

"I'll make you a deal," the guy said, giving her a wink. "Two for the price of one."

Then she saw it. Her mother's handmade gray bakery mouse clutching the silver spoon with her initials and the date she'd made it, engraved on the back.

"How about I call the cops," Andi countered, "and you explain how you stole this ornament from my cupcake shop?"

The police questioned the man for fifteen minutes, during which he claimed he'd bought the items from someone else he couldn't name. Then when some TVs and other high-dollar gifts that had been reported stolen were also found in his truck, the man was handcuffed and taken away.

"We'll let you know what we find out," an officer promised, handing her his card.

Andi turned to Jake, who had joined her once the cops started closing in. "Can you believe that guy? I hope they get him to confess he's the Grinch who's been stealing from us."

"I hope so, too," he said, an urgency tingeing his voice as they walked with the girls back to their car. "But about our move to D.C.—"

"We didn't say we'd move," Andi corrected. "And . . . I really don't want to talk about this right now."

"We *have* to talk about it," Jake said, the expression on his face anxious. "The editor of the *Post* called and said they'd prefer to hire me, but if I don't give him an answer, they'll give the job to someone else."

Andi stopped walking and met his gaze. "Okay, we'll make a decision after Christmas like we agreed."

"No." Jake gave her a solemn look. "They want to know *tonight*."

RACHEL SMILED AS she stepped over the threshold of the boutique where she and Kim had decided to shop. The beat of her heart kicked up a notch as she breathed in the scent of new clothes, sweet perfume, and the promise of another glorified purchase. She couldn't understand why anyone—*like her cousin*—wouldn't love to shop.

Okay, Kim didn't exactly share her enthusiasm either, but she had been excited to come along to find a gift for Nathaniel—which made all the difference in the world.

"Last night Nathaniel took me on a horse-drawn sleigh ride at one of the farms by Youngs River Falls, and he kept hinting he got me something special for Christmas," Kim explained. "I want to find something special for him, too, something that shows how much I care."

"I take it luggage tags are out?" Rachel teased.

"He talked to my dad," Kim said, twisting the shoulder strap of her hobo bag around and around.

"What about?"

"He won't tell me. Nathaniel said he saw my father in town, and they went for coffee. *Coffee!* Can you believe it? First I asked him if he was sure he had the right father, because my dad's never chatted with me or Andi over coffee."

Rachel frowned. "I thought you said your father had been opening up more with you and Andi over the last few months?"

"Yeah, but not enough to have a full-blown conversation. What could they possibly have talked about?"

Rachel laughed. "You look nervous. Maybe Nathaniel asked your dad for your hand in marriage. Nathaniel is a traditional kind of guy."

Kim shook her head. "Nathaniel hasn't even hinted at marriage. If anything, he keeps pressing me on my thoughts of continuous travel."

"Speaking of travel," Rachel said, picking up a pair of sunglasses from the rack in front of her. "Do you think I'll need these for Hollywood?"

Kim smirked. "Yes, in fact, I think you'll need a different set for each day of your honeymoon."

"Great idea!" Rachel agreed. "I should buy Mike some, too."

"What about your agreement?"

Rachel pictured herself with Mike in sunny California with the famed white Hollywood sign on the hill behind them. She'd wear one of those stylish wide-brimmed floppy hats she'd seen in the fashion magazines, and Mike could wear a black beret to go with his gorgeous dark brown hair. They'd each wear their sunglasses and sit under an umbrella table at a cafe sipping champagne like the movie stars.

"Oh, but he's going to love it," Rachel said. "Who can go to Hollywood without a pair of sunglasses?"

Kim looked at the price tag. "Did you know they cost a hundred dollars? You can find cheaper ones at the drugstore."

"Oh, but these are perfect," Rachel whispered. "And I've already planned the perfect wedding with a videographer, ice sculptures, a chocolate fountain, a live band, and hundreds of white rosebud flowers."

She ignored the skepticism on Kim's face and made her purchase at the cash register. "Besides, I don't have time for the drugstore," she continued, breaking into another smile. "I'm getting married tomorrow!"

RACHEL STEPPED ONTO the red-carpeted staircase with her two bridesmaids and waited for Grandpa Lewy to come give the signal that the wedding was about to start.

The historic downtown Liberty Theater, which opened in 1925 as a vaudeville/motion picture palace, had more recently been turned into an exquisite performing arts venue. She'd rented the McTavish Room, where both the ceremony and the reception would take place.

The elegant room, with its cranberry red carpets, wooden dance floor, and candlestick crystal chandelier, held 185 people, seated in groups of eight around fifteen tables. She'd calculated the numbers over and over when making her plans. Five large serving tables would be spread with the catered food, along with a buffet table for the chocolate fountain fondue and a small carving table for turkey and roast beef.

She'd waited her whole life for this once-in-a-lifetime

day. She, Rachel Marie Donovan, was about to walk down the aisle behind her most cherished friends, unite with the man she loved, and have the Cinderella wedding of her dreams.

So why were both of her bridesmaids' eyes brimming with tears? If anyone should be crying, it should be her, from sheer happiness.

"Andi, what's wrong?" she whispered. "Are you okay?"

Andi, dressed in the holly green gown her mother had been able to fix, let out a soft, audible sob. "I can't help it. I love this place."

"I love it, too," Rachel soothed. "That's why I chose to have my wedding here."

"I meant Astoria. I love Astoria. And I love Creative Cupcakes."

Rachel pretended she understood, but Andi had been acting weird, and now she was all emotional. She turned to Kim. "What about you?"

"I overheard Nathaniel talking to your cousin," Kim said, her face grim. "I thought he was flirting with her."

"Stacey?" Rachel laughed, then covered her mouth, hoping no one being seated in the other room had heard. "The woman can't even dress herself. Yesterday she wore a tie-dyed skirt and zebra print top beneath her red apron."

"He told her he plans to go away soon—to New Zealand—which is halfway around the world. He didn't mention this to me, so I doubt he intends to take me with him."

Rachel elbowed her. "Kim! Don't you see? That's what he's getting you for Christmas! Travel tickets."

Kim nodded. "But that's not what I want."

The door opened, and Grandpa Lewy, a dashing sight in his black tuxedo, looked a far cry from the sick man he'd been six months earlier. "Is there anyone here who wants to get married?"

"That's me," Rachel said, giving him a kiss on the cheek. "Are you the man they broke out of the senior center to give me away?"

Grandpa Lewy chuckled, and then a tear slipped down his cheek, too. "I'm going to miss you."

"I'm getting married," she told him. "I'm not leaving you."

He wiped his eyes. "Mike said he made an appointment to visit a real estate agent while you're down in Hollywood for your honeymoon."

Rachel hesitated. "He did?"

She only thought he suggested moving to California so she'd stop working and have babies, but now that she'd told him she'd like kids, she didn't expect to *move*.

Her flower girls, Mia and Taylor, came up the stairs to join them. They both wore white dresses and had their hair piled up on their heads with a floral circlet. Then the door opened, and one by one they all made their way down the aisle. The flowers girls went first, followed by Kim, then Andi.

The music changed, and Rachel's heart leaped into her throat. She swallowed hard, but she feared she might have to make a run for the bushes like Andi did the week before. Grandpa Lewy pulled her arm. She took a step, then looked down the long aisle and saw all eyes staring at *her*.

Mike's brother, Tristan, and his wife, Danielle, whom she'd first met at the Crab, Seafood, and Wine Festival, were there, seated next to Mike's parents. Guy Armstrong was next to her own mother—how did that happen?

Grandpa Lewy's sweetheart, Bernice, and the ladies from the Saturday Night Cupcake Club were looking back at her. The Tuesday Afternoon Romance Writers— who were saps for anything romantic, including Mistletoe Magic cupcakes—were, of course, misty-eyed. One of them had even requested permission to include them all in one of her books, and Andi had agreed.

Andi's stern-faced father and Ian Lockwell and his family were there. Their Creative Cupcakes employees, Eric, Heather, and Theresa, sat with her cousin, Stacey. And Caleb, Jake's friend from a local media crew, stood with his video camera facing her, ready to film her every expression, her every move . . .

Usually she loved the limelight. But today she wondered . . . did she spend too much money? Had she really thought all this out? Did the skirt of her gown look like a giant white tutu? Did Mike really want to move to California?

Then she saw his face. He smiled at her, and everything in the whole world seemed perfect, just as she'd imagined . . . until the lights went out.

A collective gasp filled the darkened room. Rachel couldn't see a thing. She tripped, and her grandfather must have tripped, too, because he landed on top of her.

"Rachel?"

"I'm here, Grandpa."

Someone with large feet ran past her. Another set of footsteps, lighter, rushed behind the first.

A drop of liquid fell down and splattered on her cheek, followed by another. She raised her hand to her hair and realized she was getting wet.

"Someone turn off the sprinklers!" a voice shouted.

"Where's the electric panel for the lights?" demanded another.

Rachel managed to pick up her skirt and climb back onto her feet just as a loud-ringing smoke alarm went off.

"Is there a fire?" Andi shrieked. "Mia! Taylor!"

Somewhere in all the confusion she heard Mike shout her name. "Rachel? Where are you?"

A bright beam from a flashlight circled the room, and Rachel caught sight of a figure in a Santa Claus suit hightailing it past the guests with a sack over his shoulder.

"Stop him!" her cousin shouted. "He's stealing the wedding gifts!"

The thief turned, and the flashlight illuminated a hairy green face with a large nose and sharp teeth turned upward in an evil grin.

"*Grinch!*" Taylor screamed, and her terrified cry added to the whirlwind of sound.

The flashlight fell to the ground. Rachel held onto Grandpa Lewy's arm as people around her pushed and shoved. She feared she'd trip in the dark once again, but then the overhead lights came back on.

It took another moment for her eyes to readjust, but when they did, she heard Mia cry out, "Max! How could you be so mean?"

A boy around eleven or twelve stood by the carving board, the roast beef in one hand, a Grinch mask in his other.

"Max!" Jake shouted, trying to pry Taylor's fingers off his neck. "Wait!"

But the boy cringed, dropped the items in both hands beside the Santa suit on the ground, and ran for the door.

Andi hurried to Jake's side. "Your Max and Mia's imaginary friend are the same?"

Rachel handed Grandpa Lewy off to her mother and searched for Mike. She couldn't see him, so she moved closer to Jake and Andi.

"Why would he do this?" Jake asked.

"Because Santa never brings Max presents," Mia explained.

Mia's blond hair stuck up out of her floral circlet in a discombobulated puff, and Rachel suddenly wondered what her own hair looked like. What about her dress? What about her flowers? *What about her wedding?*

"Who had the flashlight?" Andi asked.

Stacey stepped forward. "Me. I always carry one in my purse in case there's . . . trouble."

The devastation and the reality of the situation suddenly became clear, and Rachel couldn't contain her Irish temper. "Why is there always trouble whenever you're around?"

Stacey flinched. "This isn't *my* fault."

Mike, dressed in his black tuxedo with a mistletoe boutonniere, pushed through the crowd and found her.

"Rachel, are you all right?" he asked, taking her arm.

"Oh, Mike! Our wedding is ruined!"

"It doesn't have to be. We can still get married."

"What about the boy who ran off?"

"Officer Lockwell called the station, and the police are already looking for him."

"Did you see what he did!" she exclaimed. "The tables are overturned, the food is destroyed; look at my chocolate fondue fountain all over the floor. Look at *me*—I'm all wet! And our gifts are gone. Oh, no! I bet he even took the wedding gift I had for you."

"You bought me a gift? I thought we agreed not to buy each other gifts." Mike stared at her. "We never needed any of this stuff to get married. Who needs ice sculptures and chocolate fountains, anyway? How much did all this cost?"

"Worried we won't have enough to move to Hollywood?" she countered. "When were you going to tell me you planned to look at housing in California?"

Mike did a double-take. "We already talked about it when we agreed we should sell the shop for the one point two million."

Andi's mouth dropped open. "You want to sell the shop?"

"It might be a good idea," Jake told them, "now that I got a job with the *Washington Post* and Andi and I are moving to Washington, D.C."

Andi shook her head. "But when Mr. Pennyworth called back with another offer, I turned him down."

"What?" Rachel demanded, hands on her hips. "Kim, did you know about this?"

"I don't want to move!" Andi said. "I'm only doing it for Jake."

Jake's eyes widened, shock written all over his face, then he set his jaw. "I'm going after Max."

A moment later he was gone.

"What's wrong with you?" Kim screeched. "Andi? Rachel? You two were the ones who dragged me into the cupcake shop with you, and now I'm the only one who wants to stay?"

"Kimberly, you could travel," Nathaniel said, placing a hand on her shoulder from behind.

Kim spun around. "Don't you get it? I don't want to travel all the time. I love to travel, yes, but I want roots, a home, kids, a family."

"You do?" Nathaniel's mouth dropped open. "But I thought—"

"Did you see that young boy?" Kim said, pointing to the door. "Kids need a place they can call home."

Kim, too, ran for the door, and Rachel threw her hands into the air. "The wedding is a disaster!"

"No, it's not," Mike told her. "Rachel, *we're* still here. What's more important—all your perfect party plans or me?"

Rachel shook her head. "We can't get married like this."

Mike hesitated, then nodded, his expression hard. "You know what? You're right—we can't."

Mike stalked off behind everyone else exiting the building, and Rachel collapsed onto the floor, her dress encasing her in a heap of damp, satin-and-lace fluff.

Andi glanced back and forth between them. "Rachel, you have to go after him."

Rachel looked up and met her gaze. "And what would I say?"

"Tell him there's always hope," Mia said, tugging on Andi's hand. "C'mon, Mom, we have to find Max! No one should be alone on Christmas."

Chapter Nine

One of the most glorious messes in the world is
the mess created in the living room on Christmas
Day. Don't clean it up too quickly.

—Andy Rooney

KIM WALKED DOWN the street toward Creative Cupcakes
not knowing what the day would bring. One thing was
for sure: there hadn't been any sugarplums dancing in
her head Christmas Eve.

Nathaniel hadn't called, or maybe he had, but her cell
phone got wet at the Liberty Theater, and now it wasn't
working. She didn't want to talk, anyway, or she would
have borrowed a phone and called him.

For all she knew, he was halfway around the world by
now. The handsome, blue-eyed, blond-haired Swede left

his last girlfriend because she didn't like to travel, and he didn't want to be tied down. Now that she'd told him she didn't want to be a globe-trotter either, it was possible Nathaniel had hopped the first plane to Sweden to spend Christmas with his family.

The streets were quiet, only one passing car. She imagined most people were just waking up, running to their stockings, opening gifts. Andi had gifts and stocking stuffers tucked away for Mia and Taylor, but they had planned to meet at the cupcake shop for their main celebration. *If* anyone still felt like celebrating. *Merry Christmas, indeed!*

She turned the corner and stopped short when she saw Rachel and Andi, Mia, and Taylor standing in front of their shop.

"Your pictures are back," Mia called to her.

Kim drew closer and looked at the Christmas images painted on the window. The Grinch was gone, and someone had tried to duplicate the stocking, the tree, and the blue-buttoned snowman she had painted on there before. But it wasn't the same. The brushstrokes had Max's signature style written all over them. Did he feel guilty about what he'd done? Was this his way of trying to make amends?

The strands of Christmas lights, wreath, and jingle bells on the door had also been replaced, and Frosty, patched with duct tape, had been reinflated.

"Frosty came back to life on Christmas Day," Mia said with a big smile, "just like he did in the cartoon on TV."

Taylor clapped her hands. "Santa Claus must have come to the cupcake shop to drop him off!"

Kim pulled on a smile for the girls' sake. "What did Santa bring you for Christmas?"

"I got a new doll," Taylor said excitedly. "She walks and talks and can even ride a horse."

"How about you, Mia?"

"I got a new sled, a video game, and some other stuff, but Santa didn't bring as many presents this year. No Easy-Bake Oven."

Andi cringed. "Maybe he didn't have any left."

Kim looked at Rachel, who remained silent. "Are you okay?"

Rachel shrugged. "Are you?"

Kim shook her head. "I don't think I'm getting a ring."

"I don't think I'm getting married!" Rachel wailed.

Andi broke into tears. "I think I might be headed for a second divorce! Jake didn't come home last night."

Then all at once Kim ran toward them, and she, Rachel, and Andi were all hugging and crying and apologizing to each other.

"I'm so sorry," Andi said, wiping her eyes. "I should have told you about the second offer on the shop and Jake's job offer in Washington, D.C."

"I should have told you we wanted to sell and that Mike wants us to live in California," Rachel admitted.

"I should have told you Nathaniel wanted me to use the money to take a year off and travel the world," Kim added.

"We're *all* the Grinch," Andi declared. "We need to

grow bigger hearts and promise to be honest with each other."

"Agreed," Rachel and Kim said in unison.

WHEN THEY ENTERED the shop, Andi took their golden cupcake cutter off the wall and a salted caramel cupcake out of the glass display case.

"All for one, one for all," Andi said solemnly. "This is how we started. Together. And I think we need a cupcake to help us figure out what we want."

Kim hesitated. "But it isn't any of our birthdays."

"Who cares?" Andi replied, splitting the cupcake three ways. "When we're in despair and need to brainstorm, this is what we do."

"I don't want to sell the shop," Kim told them.

"Me either," Rachel agreed. "If Mike and I have babies, I want to raise them in Astoria, close to our families."

"So do I," Andi said, with a catch in her voice. "But Jake wants to move."

"No, he doesn't." Jake came up behind Andi and kissed her neck. Then he nodded toward the cupcake in the center of the table. "Aren't you going to cut that cupcake in four? I *am* your partner, you know."

Kim smiled. Her sister got lucky when she met Jake. He really loved her.

"I forgot why I wanted to invest in this cupcake shop in the first place," Jake said, giving Andi's shoulder a squeeze. "My job at the newspaper wasn't enough. I wanted a connection, to be a part of a team, to have a family again—like when I was young and my family ran the pizzeria."

"What about your job offer?" Andi asked.

Jake grinned. "While I was out last night looking for Max, I called the *Post* editor and told him my decision."

Kim thought of the boy alone on the streets and leaned forward. "And Max?"

"Still missing," Jake replied. "But he isn't the Grinch."

Jake unfolded the newspaper in his hand and showed them the front page of the *Astoria Sun*.

They all leaned their heads in, and Kim read, "*FOUND! THE GRINCH WHO STOLE CHRISTMAS!*"

"The cops caught Max's foster father, Garth Gilmore, with Rachel and Mike's wedding cards and gifts late last night," Jake explained. "The guy they arrested in Ilwaco told them where to find him."

"Why would he do something like this?" Rachel demanded.

"Garth tried to sell the gifts to last-minute shoppers," Jake told them. "He had some of the gifts he stole from the Cupcake Mobile, too."

Andi frowned. "How did he know they were in there?"

"My fault," Jake admitted. "During the interview, I told Garth we were collecting gifts for foster children. I asked if we could put Max's name on the list. When Garth came to steal from the shop, he must have looked in the truck and seen the presents under the blanket. Then he saw the Grinch painted on our window and decided to steal the name."

Rachel looked puzzled. "Who painted the Grinch on the window?"

"Max," Kim answered. "I met him at the school touching up the murals. His mother used to waitress here when this place was still Zeke's Tavern."

Jake nodded. "Then when Garth stole the gifts out of the Cupcake Mobile, he saw all the Christmas decorations and the gifts we had for each other inside the shop and decided to come back and steal them, too."

"And he saw the details for my wedding cake in the Cupcake Diary!" Rachel exclaimed. "He knew the wedding's location, date, and time."

"Your perfect wedding was too perfect for him to pass up," Kim added.

Andi raised her eyebrows. "Then what was Max doing there?"

"Trying to stop him." Jake shook his head. "I wish I knew where he was."

Rachel sighed. "I wish I knew where Mike was."

The connecting door to the back party room opened, and Mike appeared. "I'm right here."

For a moment no one moved. Then Kim looked at Rachel and found Andi and Jake did the same.

Rachel rose from the table. "I'm sorry, Mike. I went overboard on the wedding when I promised you I wouldn't, and—"

"I never should have expected you to continue the wedding after everything that happened." Mike crossed the room. "I think *I'm* the Grinch. How could I not understand how you must have felt at that moment? Or how you felt about moving?"

"Do you know how I feel now?" Rachel asked, a smile spreading across her face.

"You want to reschedule the wedding?" Mike asked, his expression hopeful.

"Yes," Rachel said. "I do. Will you marry me now?"

Kim couldn't help but laugh at Mike's expression.

"Now?" Mike repeated. "What about your ice sculptures, chocolate fountains, crystal chandeliers, and fancy dress?"

"You were right," Rachel told him. "I don't need any of those things. All I need is you."

Oh, no! Kim didn't think she was going to be able to hold it together, not after Andi and Jake's happy reunion, and now theirs, too.

Rachel ran into Mike's arms, and Kim had to turn away as they kissed. She couldn't stop the envy from cutting deep into her heart. But as she looked out the front window, she saw a boy watching them, his face up against the glass.

She pointed. "There he is!"

Everyone turned toward the window and chorused, *"Who? Who?"*

The boy must have seen their reactions because he sprang back.

"Max!" Kim ran to the window. "He ran off again. Where would he go?"

"To the bus station?" Rachel suggested.

Andi glanced at Jake. "Or the train station?"

"He must have run because I said he was mean, but I didn't know he wasn't the Grinch," Mia said, all in one breath.

"Mia," Andi said, kneeling down to her daughter's level. "Do you know where Max might go?"

"Maybe Hawaii. His mom gave him a picture of Hawaii."

Jake snapped his fingers. "The marina. He plans to stow away on a boat. I'm going after him."

Andi nodded. "Me, too. Rachel and Mike, can you watch the girls?"

"Me three," Kim said. "I want to help search."

She turned toward the door and ran smack into a tall figure she didn't realize had been standing there. *Nathaniel.*

He gave her a hesitant look. "Can I come with you?"

MAX DIDN'T STOP running until he got to the waterfront. Christmas Day, the place was empty. There was no trolley, there were no cannery workers, no one to see him climb aboard a boat. He'd hide under the deck in the cabin, maybe lie under a tarp or crawl into a cabinet when the fishermen came the next day to sail out to sea.

Maybe he could convince them to let him join the crew until he turned eighteen. Or maybe he'd jump ship and get off at another port and make his way . . . North? South? Where would his mother have gone?

Didn't matter. She didn't want him. He kind of figured she wasn't coming back, but to hear Jake say it made him so mad. How could she lie to him? How could she leave him?

He couldn't spend another six years in foster care. The people his social worker placed him with were like the sea lions, known as "Astoria's losers." They lay around, ate, and barked complaints all day. They smelled bad, too.

Worse, the big sea lions were protected by the fish and wildlife organization even though they ate the salmon—which were also supposed to be protected.

Yup, a whole lot like foster care.

He thought of Mia as he ran down the dock. He wished he'd kept the magician's cape she had given him. The air outside was cold. Sharp. Ice crystals fell on his head, making his ears sting. He covered them with his hands.

After a quick scan of the boats, he chose the one on the end, the one with the most cover. He climbed over the side and dropped in. Then his stomach growled, and the image in his mind of the hot, juicy hunk of meat he'd pulled away from Garth at the Liberty Theater made him hungrier.

He'd suspected Garth was the gift-stealing Grinch Mia told him about when the guy came home with the Santa suit and Grinch mask. Garth had already stolen the gift his social worker had given him and sold it to a vendor on the street corner. Why wouldn't he steal the gifts for the other children?

When Garth went out that night, Max followed him to the Liberty Theater. He'd hidden behind a curtain and watched as Garth messed with the switches in the metal box on the wall. Then the lights had gone out, and he couldn't see much until someone had turned on a flashlight. That's when he saw Garth steal the wedding gifts, the rolls off the serving table, and the slab of turkey. When Garth had made a grab for the roast beef, Max lunged forward and pulled it out of his reach.

He didn't know Mia's family was at the wedding, or that he'd get caught holding the roast, until the overhead lights came back on. The police must be looking for him. They probably thought *he* was the thief.

Jake and Mia did.

Chapter Ten

Wouldn't life be worth the living,
Wouldn't dreams be coming true,
If we kept the Christmas spirit,
All the whole year through?

—*Author unknown*

ANDI SQUINTED THROUGH the snow as she scanned the boats docked along the waterfront. The problem with Astoria was that it was surrounded by water on three sides, with hundreds of boats Max could be hiding in.

Kim and Nathaniel split off to search the West Mooring Basin Marina on the other end of town, while she and Jake stayed here on the east end.

"Max!" Jake called.

No answer.

"I think I understand how he feels," Andi said as they searched another dock. "There were many times when I wanted to run away from my father."

"At least you had people to call family, and despite your differences, you knew they would be there. Some kids, like Max, have no one."

A shuffle rattled the boat to Andi's left. "Jake, listen!"

Together they drew toward one of the pilot boats used by the Coast Guard to lead cargo ships through the trouble spots of the Columbia River.

Jake swung one leg over the side and looked around. "Max! We're here to help. We know it wasn't you who took the gifts."

Andi pointed toward the cabin, where she heard another shuffle. Jake nodded and moving forward, pulled a blue tarp off the deck. Still nothing.

"The police arrested Garth," Jake said, raising his voice. "If you come with us, we'll give you a place to stay, warm clothes, food—"

"Stay—with *you*?" asked a small voice.

Jake pulled a pile of ropes apart, and the boy Andi had seen at the wedding sat shivering beneath. Jake took off his coat and wrapped it around his shoulders.

"Thank God you're okay," Jake told him. "Do you know how long I've been out here looking for you? We have to get you back to the shop where I can give you your present."

"You got me a present?" Max asked wide-eyed.

"Mia made you one, too," Andi said with a smile, "but you'll have to come with us to see what it is."

Max looked as if he weren't sure he could trust her. "I was the one who painted the Grinch on your window. Garth sold the gift my social worker gave me for a carton of cigarettes, and . . . I was mad."

"I would have been mad, too," Andi told him. "But I wouldn't have deflated Frosty, taken away anyone's Christmas lights, or painted over anyone's decorations."

Max nodded. "I'm sorry. I tried to put it all back."

"I know." Andi smiled. "We forgive you."

"But . . . I *stole* from you," he spat out. "Just like Garth. What I did was wrong."

"We all mess up," she said as he and Jake climbed out of the boat and back onto the dock. "Every single one of us. But Christmas is about giving and forgiving, and the chance to make relationships right. We'd like to give you that chance, Max. Will you celebrate Christmas with us?"

The boy glanced between her and Jake, then nodded. "If Mia made me a present, she'd be disappointed if I didn't come."

"*We'd* be disappointed, too, Max," Jake told him. He put his arm around Max's shoulders as they left the boat behind.

WHEN THEY ARRIVED back at the shop, Rachel's mother, cousin, and church pastor were there, along with Mike's parents and Guy Armstrong. Kim and Nathaniel had already returned, and everyone greeted Max with enthusiasm.

"Max," Kim said, giving him a hug. "I'm so glad they found you!"

The boy looked embarrassed by all the attention.

"I know you aren't a Grinch," Mia told him. "The real Grinch could steal gifts out of our shop without a key. I think he shrunk himself like an ant and crawled through the keyhole."

"No," Max said, as he looked around at all their faces. "He came up through the trapdoor in the party room."

"Trapdoor?" Andi asked, sucking in her breath. "Where? Can you show us?"

Max led them to the back room that had once been Guy's tattoo parlor and pried up a loose square section of floorboard. "The room below has a tunnel that leads out toward the river. In the old days the pirates and sea captains would kidnap people from the tavern, bring them through here, and force them to join their crew."

Andi nodded. "They were shanghaied, just like the people at the Captain's Port."

"They're the only two buildings in Astoria that still have passages," Max informed them. "There was one more up the hill from the bridge, but the tunnel is all closed in now."

"In all the years I worked in this room, I never knew the trapdoor was there," Guy said, his eyes glued to the gaping hole.

"How did Garth know it was here?" Jake asked.

"My social worker told him I used to play under there while my mom worked. She was a waitress when this place was Zeke's Tavern, and one of the sailors told her about the trapdoor." Max made a sour face and shrugged. "She didn't have money for a babysitter. When her boss found out about me, she was fired and . . . that's when she went away."

Beside her, Andi overheard Rachel whisper, "Do you think *I'll* make a good mom?"

"Someday, when we do have kids," Mike assured her, "you'll be stupendous."

"The cops never found the gifts stolen from our shop," Jake said, moving toward the open passage. "Do you think they could still be down here?"

"Yes!" Kim said, peering into the hole. "I see them! Garth probably planned to sell them at a later date."

While Max went with Rachel and Mike in the Cupcake Mobile to help deliver the packages to all the local foster kids, Andi and Kim stayed behind to decorate the shop.

"Lucky for Rachel the pastor could celebrate with us today," Andi said, mixing the batter for a new wedding cake. "He said he would marry them as soon as they get back."

"Do you think they'll get married in the Santa and Mrs. Claus costumes they're wearing?" Kim teased.

Andi laughed. "No. Rachel's mom cleaned and pressed Rachel's Cinderella dress and Mike's tuxedo, but it's a surprise."

Two hours later, the lemon chiffon pudding cupcakes iced with creamy white vanilla frosting and sprinkled with clear sugar crystals were stacked into the shape of a beautiful white Christmas tree.

Andi placed her mother's handmade bakery mouse ornament back on their real tree with the macaroni angels, cranberry garlands, and fresh popcorn strings.

Kim and Nathaniel hadn't actually made up, but it looked like they'd formed a temporary truce as they decorated the shop together. Nathaniel brought in wreaths, poinsettias, and a large bouquet of white roses for Rachel's bridal bouquet. Kim rehung the stockings, tied ribbons and bows to all of the chairs, and placed jingle bells around candy cane favors.

"Hot guy alert!" Kim announced as she passed by.

Andi looked up. "Where?"

"Under the mistletoe kissing Rachel's cousin."

The young man was one of Mike's relatives who flew in for the wedding.

Guy Armstrong narrowed his gaze and pressed his lips together. "Okay, I'm going to see once and for all if this thing really works."

He waited until Stacey and her man moved off to a corner, then took their place under the mistletoe that Nathaniel had hung near the entrance of the front door.

After a few minutes he scowled. "See? Doesn't work."

Andi and Kim exchanged a big smile as Sarah came through the door carrying Rachel's and Mike's wedding clothes. She set the garment bags on a hook, then tiptoed up behind Guy and placed her hands over his eyes. "Guess who?"

"Someone who will give me a kiss?" he asked.

Sarah didn't answer but turned him around with a smile and gave in to his request.

When Guy opened his eyes, he looked at her and grinned. "Okay, maybe mistletoe has some magic in it after all."

A short while later Rachel, Mike, and Max returned, their faces aglow.

"The kids were so excited," Max reported.

"Yes, they were," Rachel agreed. "Almost as excited as I am to finally get married!"

Sarah presented her with her dress, and they hugged. Then when Rachel and Mike saw all the preparations, they hugged each other and vowed to race to the make-shift dressing room in the kitchen pantry.

RACHEL AND MIKE stood by the Christmas tree, gazed into each other's eyes, and pledged their lives to each other in the simplicity of their Creative Cupcakes shop. Andi had never been part of anything so beautiful, except for her own wedding.

Beside her, Kim squeezed her bouquet of mistletoe tight, even tighter during the ring exchange. She and Nathaniel were still circling each other like wary strangers, which made it all the more awkward when Rachel tossed her bouquet, and Kim caught it.

Andi could almost feel the dread emanating from Kim's expression, and her heart went out to her. The trepidation multiplied ten times more when Mike threw the garter, the other men stepped out of the way, and Nathaniel was the only man left standing.

Folktales stated that the single girl and single guy who caught the bridal ware would be the next in line to marry. But Andi knew Kim believed that—in *this* case, they couldn't have gotten it more wrong.

"Do I really have to go through with this?" Kim whispered.

Andi squeezed her hand. "Oh, Kim! I'm so sorry!"

Kim's cheeks turned red. As was tradition, she was going to have to face Nathaniel, allow him to slide the garter up her leg, and pretend she was fine.

Kim sat in the chair Mike had brought to the center of the room, and Nathaniel stepped forward, garter in hand. Then Nathaniel took a deep breath, and Andi got the impression he was as nervous as her sister.

He kneeled, lifted the floor-length hem of Kim's holly green Christmas skirt, and slipped the garter over her toe, up her calf, and over her knee.

"Kim," Nathaniel said, "open your eyes."

Andi could tell her sister hadn't wanted to look, but when she did, Kim let out a scream.

What happened? Andi craned her neck to see and almost screamed herself when she spotted the glittering diamond ring tied around the blue lace garter.

"That was fast!" Rachel exclaimed, an even bigger smile spreading over her already smiling face.

"Kimberly Nicole Burke," Nathaniel said, taking the ring off the garter and transferring it to her hand, "I love you. The greatest adventure I could ever have would be to share my life with you. I want a home, family, and kids, all of it."

"You do?" Kim didn't look like she believed him.

"Why do you think I committed to buying the garden nursery? I've traveled enough to know that this is where I'd like to establish a permanent residence. But then I met you and I was afraid that *you* were the one who would want as many stamps as you could fit in your passport."

Kim, not usually one to give in to emotion, was a teary mess. "I heard you tell Stacey about your travel plans to New Zealand."

"I told her I thought it would make a good honeymoon destination—with you."

Kim laughed. "I can do honeymoons."

Nathaniel grinned. "Is that a yes? *Ja*? Will you marry me?"

"Yes!" Kim shouted and flung her arms around him for a kiss. "I love you, too!"

"A few minutes earlier, and we could have made it a double wedding," Mike joked.

Rachel walked over and apologized to her cousin. "If you didn't shine the light on the Grinch, no one would have seen him. You win the reward of a dozen peppermint hot chocolate cupcakes."

Stacey gave only a half-smile.

"If she doesn't want them, I'll take them," Grandpa Lewy said, leaning in.

"Too bad you have to leave, Stacey," Rachel added. "You've been a great help in the kitchen."

"Actually," Stacey told them, "I don't have . . . anywhere to go. In Coeur d'Alene I stayed with a friend but couldn't find a job, and . . . now I'm homeless and flat broke."

"You can be the one who runs our new traveling cupcake stand on the beach this summer," Andi told her.

"What cupcake stand?" Rachel and Kim demanded.

"The one we'll buy with the money my dead-beat ex

finally paid me back with after all these years," Andi said, barely able to hold on to her excitement.

"Should we open the gifts?" Jake asked, motioning everyone together.

Rachel and Mike admitted they did have a gift for each other. Homemade gifts. Mike presented Rachel with a miniature model of the cupcake shop. Rachel gave him hand-written movie tickets for a quiet night of popcorn and romance at home.

Kim gave Nathaniel a canvas she had painted of two turtle doves perched on top of the Astoria Column, nose to nose as if they were kissing. And he gave her a rose garden of her very own, in his yard, with her name on it so that there would be no doubt in the future where she belonged.

Andi watched the excitement cross Mia's face as she opened one of the gifts they'd pulled up through the trapdoor.

"An Easy-Bake Oven!" her daughter squealed. Then Mia handed a stocking to Max, the same one she'd written his name on with glitter.

"A friendship bracelet," Max said, pulling out the bright purple-and-pink braided band. "Uh ... thanks, Mia. They're my favorite colors."

Mike's mother, who no one knew very well, leaned toward Max, and Andi heard her say, "You've got your father's brown hair and your mother's blue eyes."

Max flushed and glanced at her and Jake. Then shook his head. "They're not my parents."

The lady shrugged. "They look as if they *could* be."

Andi turned her head and caught Jake looking at her. "Are you thinking what I'm thinking?"

"Adopt Max?" Jake asked and nodded.

"My father is going to say I'm being impulsive again. What will I tell him?"

Jake grinned. "That you were moved by compassion."

"He says it's my compassion that gets me into trouble."

"And I say it's your compassion that I love most about you. Tell him it's my idea, and we can be impulsive together."

Jake motioned to the stocking in Max's hands. "There's something else for you in there."

Max lifted out a pair of new drumsticks. "No way! For me?"

"The tag says, 'Love, Santa,'" Mia said, pointing to the words. "He found you this year."

"Goes with your other gift in the kitchen," Jake told him. "What's a drumstick without a drum?"

Max stared at him, ran into the kitchen with Mia, gave a whoop of delight, and ran back. "What's the catch?"

"No catch," Jake said, "but an offer. You don't need to be a rock star to be somebody special. If you agree to join our family, you will be special to us."

Max frowned. "I don't understand."

"Will you adopt us?" Jake asked. "Although I must warn you before you make a decision—you'd also be gaining two sisters."

Andi touched Jake's arm and smiled. "Actually, he'd be gaining one more, but I'm not sure if it's a girl or a boy."

Jake opened his mouth and stared at her. Then finally said, "You're . . . you're—"

Andi nodded. "We're having a baby."

"She gave me a baby for Christmas!" Jake shouted.

"We're going to need a bigger house," Andi told him.

"After we all get back from Hawaii," Jake agreed and held up five airline tickets.

Andi gasped. "How did you know to get five?"

"Well, one was supposed to be for your father, but we don't have to tell him that."

"What do you say, Max?" Andi asked, holding her breath. "Will you accept this crazy family as your own?"

The bright smile that spread across Max's face lit up the whole room. "I will!"

After Max ran back to his drum set, Andi wrapped her arms around Jake's neck and pulled him close. "What if I told you that you're the most caring person I've ever met?"

"What if I told you I've never loved anyone as much as I love you?" He grinned. "Except . . . Taylor, Mia, our new baby, and now Max—"

Andi laughed, her heart happy and full. "I'd say this is the best Christmas ever. And love . . . is the best gift."

"A gift we can use all year long."

She smiled. "And can't be stolen."

Jake leaned down and captured her lips in a sweet, passionate, head-swirling kiss. Then Andi looked around the circle of people holding hands and singing carols, with their holiday Scrooge standing on a chair in the middle. Her eyes narrowed. What was he up to? Was that a smile on his face? A sparkle of holiday joy?

"Merry Christmas!" Guy Armstrong shouted. "Cupcakes for all! And God bless us, everyone!"

Recipe for
PEPPERMINT HOT CHOCOLATE CUPCAKES

from Malorie Gibson of Jackson, New Jersey

www.SweetBumCupcakes.com

Cupcake Ingredients:

2 cups flour

2 cups sugar

½ cup unsweetened cocoa powder

1½ teaspoons baking soda

1 ½ cups milk

½ cup butter

1 teaspoon vanilla

1 teaspoon peppermint extract

2 eggs

Instructions:

Preheat oven to 350 degrees.

Measure out everything except the eggs directly into your mixer bowl.

Mix on low speed until incorporated. Continue to beat on high speed for 2 minutes.

Add eggs, beat on high speed for another 2 minutes.

Cook 15–20 minutes until a toothpick comes out clean.

Ganache Ingredients:

½ cup heavy cream

¼ teaspoons vanilla

8 ounces good semisweet chocolate chips

Instructions:

Bring heavy cream and vanilla to a boil, then stir in chocolate chips until melted and remove from heat. Let sit for about an hour until ready to be put in the middle of the cupcake.

Frosting Ingredients:

   2 sticks butter
   ½ cup cocoa
   1 cups confectioner's sugar
   1 teaspoon vanilla
   1 teaspoon peppermint extract
   3 cups confectioner's sugar

Instructions:

Beat butter on high for about 30 seconds until soft.

Add cocoa and 1 cup of sugar and beat until incorporated.

Add vanilla, peppermint, and 3 cups of sugar and beat until incorporated.

After cupcakes are cooked and cooled, take a knife and cut a hole in the middle of the cupcake (reserve the top), pour or spoon the ganache in the middle of the cupcake, and replace the top. Frost the top of the cupcake and garnish with some chopped peppermint candies if desired. Enjoy!

*Keep reading for excerpts from the first three
books in The Cupcake Diaries series,*

SWEET ON YOU, RECIPE FOR LOVE,

and

TASTE OF ROMANCE,

now available from Avon Impulse.

An Excerpt from

THE CUPCAKE DIARIES: SWEET ON YOU

Forget love . . . I'd rather fall in chocolate!

—Author unknown

ANDI CAST A glance over the rowdy karaoke crowd to the man sitting at the front table with the clear plastic bakery box in his possession.

"What am I supposed to say?" she whispered, looking back at her sister, Kim, and their friend Rachel as the three of them huddled together. "Can I have your cupcake? He'll think I'm a lunatic."

"Say 'please,' and tell him about our tradition," Kim suggested.

"Offer him money." Rachel dug through her dilapidated Gucci knockoff purse and withdrew a ten-dollar bill. "And let him know we're celebrating your sister's birthday."

"You did promise me a cupcake for my birthday," Kim said with an impish grin. "Besides, the guy doesn't look like he plans to eat it. He hasn't even glanced at the cupcake since the old woman came in and delivered the box."

Andi tucked a loose strand of her dark blond hair behind her ear and drew in a deep breath. She wasn't used to taking food from anyone. Usually she was on the other end—giving it away. Her fault. She didn't plan ahead.

Why couldn't any of the businesses here be open twenty-four hours like in Portland? Out of the two dozen eclectic cafes and restaurants along the Astoria waterfront promising to satisfy customers' palates, shouldn't at least one cater to late-night customers like herself? No, they all shut down at 10:30, some earlier, as if they knew she was coming. That's what she got for living in a small town. Anticipation but no cake.

However, she was determined not to let her younger sister down. She'd promised Kim a cupcake for her twenty-sixth birthday, and she'd try her best to procure one, even if it meant making a fool of herself.

Andi shot her ever-popular friend Rachel a wry look. "You know you're better at this than I am."

Rachel grinned. "You're going to have to start interacting with the opposite sex again sometime."

Maybe. But not on the personal level, Rachel's tone suggested. Andi's divorce the previous year had left behind a bitter aftertaste no amount of sweet talk could dissolve.

Pushing back her chair, she stood up. "Tonight, all I want is the cupcake."

ANDI HAD TAKEN only a few steps when the man with the bakery box turned his head and smiled.

He probably thought she was coming over, hoping to find a date. Why shouldn't he? The Captain's Port was filled with people looking for a connection, if not for a lifetime, then at least for the hour or so they shared within the friendly confines of the restaurant's casual, communal atmosphere.

She hesitated midstep before continuing forward. Heat rushed into her cheeks. Dressed in jeans and a navy blue tie and sport jacket, he was even better looking than she'd first thought. Thirtyish. Light brown hair, fair skin with an evening shadow along his jaw, and the most amazing gold-flecked, chocolate brown eyes she'd ever seen. *Oh my.* He could have his pick of any woman in the place. Any woman in Astoria, Oregon.

"Hi," he said.

Andi swallowed the nervous tension gathering at the back of her throat and managed a smile in return. "Hi. I'm sorry to bother you, but it's my sister's birthday, and I promised her a cupcake." She nodded toward the see-through box and waved the ten-dollar bill. "Is there any chance I can persuade you to sell the one you have here?"

His brows shot up. "You want my cupcake?"

"I meant to bake a batch this afternoon," she gushed, her words tumbling over themselves, "but I ended up packing spring break lunches for the needy kids in the school district. Have you heard of the Kids' Coalition backpack program?"

He nodded. "Yes, I think the *Astoria Sun* featured the free lunch backpack program on the community page a few weeks ago."

"I'm a volunteer," she explained. "And after I finished, I tried to buy a cupcake but didn't get to the store in time. I've never let my sister down before, and I feel awful."

The new addition to her list of top ten dream-worthy males leaned back in his chair and pressed his lips together, as if considering her request, then shook his head. "I'd love to help you, but—"

"*Please.*" Andi gasped, appalled she'd stooped to begging. She straightened her shoulders and lifted her chin. "I understand if you can't, it's just that my sister, Kim, my friend Rachel, and I have a tradition."

"What kind of tradition?"

Andi pointed to their table, and Kim and Rachel smiled and waved. "Our birthdays are spaced four months apart, so we split a celebration cupcake three ways and set new goals for ourselves from one person's birthday to the next. It's easier than trying to set goals for an entire year."

"I don't suppose you could set your goals without the cupcake?" he asked, his eyes sparkling with amusement.

Andi smiled. "It wouldn't be the same."

"If the cupcake were mine to give, it would be yours. But this particular cupcake was delivered for a research project I have at work."

"Wish I had your job." Andi dropped into the chair he pulled out for her and placed her hands flat on the table. "What if I told you it's been a really tough day, tough week, tough year?"

He pushed his empty coffee cup aside, and the corners of his mouth twitched upward. "I'd say I could argue the same."

"But did you spend the last three hours running all over town looking for a cupcake?" she challenged, playfully mimicking Rachel's flirtatious, sing-song tone. "The Pig 'n Pancake was closed, along with the supermarket, and the cafe down the street said they don't even sell them anymore. And then . . . I met you."

He covered her left hand with his own, and although the unexpected contact made her jump, she ignored the impulse to pull her fingers away. His gesture seemed more an act of compassion than anything else, and, frankly, she liked the feel of his firm yet gentle touch.

"What if I told you," he said, leaning forward, "that I've traveled five hundred and seventy miles and waited sixty-three days to taste this one cupcake?"

Andi leaned toward him as well. "I'd say that's ridiculous. There's no cupcake in Astoria worth all that trouble."

"What if this particular cupcake isn't from Astoria?"

"No?" She took another look at the box but didn't see a label. "Where's it from?"

"Hollande's French Pastry Parlor outside of Portland."

"What if I told you I would send you a dozen Hollande's cupcakes tomorrow?"

"What if I told *you*," he said, and stopped to release a deep, throaty chuckle, "this is the last morsel of food I have to eat before I starve to death today?"

Andi laughed. "I'd say that's a good way to go. Or I could invite you to my place and cook you dinner."

Her heart stopped, stunned by her own words, then rebooted a moment later when their gazes locked, and he smiled at her.

"You can have the cupcake on one condition."

"Which is?"

Giving her a wink, he slid the bakery box toward her. Then he leaned his head in close and whispered in her ear.

An Excerpt from

THE CUPCAKE DIARIES: RECIPE FOR LOVE

Life is uncertain. Eat dessert first.

—Ernestine Ulmer

RACHEL PUSHED THROUGH the double doors of the kitchen, took one look at the masked man at the counter, and dropped the freshly baked tray of cupcakes on the floor.

Did he plan to rob Creative Cupcakes, demand she hand over the money from the cash register? Her eyes darted around the frilly pink-and-white shop. The loud clang of the metal bakery pan hitting the tile had caused several customers sitting at the tables to glance in her direction. Would the masked man threaten the other people as well? How could she protect them?

She stepped over the white-frosted chocolate mess by

her feet, tried to judge the distance to the telephone on the wall, and turned her attention back to the masked man before her. Maybe he wasn't a robber but someone dressed for a costume party or play. The man with the black masquerade mask covering the upper half of his face also wore a black cape.

"If this is a holdup, you picked the wrong place, Zorro." She tossed her fiery red curls over her shoulder with false bravado and laid a protective hand across the old bell-ringing register. "We don't have any money."

His hazel eyes gleamed through the holes in the mask, and he flashed her a disarming smile. "Maybe I can help with that."

He turned his hand to show an empty palm, and relief flooded over her. No gun. Then he closed his fingers and swung his fist around in the air three times. When he opened his palm again, he held a quarter, which he tossed in her direction.

Rachel caught the coin and laughed. "You're a magician."

"Mike the Magnificent," he said, extending his cape wide with one arm and taking a bow. "I'm here for the Lockwell party."

Rachel pointed to the door leading to the back party room. The space had originally been a tattoo shop, but the tattoo artist relocated to the rental next door. "The Lockwells aren't here yet. The party doesn't start until three."

"I came early to set up before the kids arrive," Mike told her. "Can't have them discovering my secrets."

"No, I guess not," Rachel agreed. "If they did, Mike the magician might not be so magnificent."

"Magnificence is hard to maintain." His lips twitched, as if suppressing a grin. "Are you Andi?"

She shook her head. "Rachel, Creative Cupcakes' stupendous co-owner, baker, and promoter."

This time a grin did escape his mouth, which led her to notice his strong, masculine jawline.

"Tell me, Rachel, what is it that makes you so stupendous?"

She gave him her most flirtatious smile. "Sorry, I can't reveal my secrets either."

"Afraid if I found out the truth, I might not think you're so impressively great?"

Rachel froze, fearing Mike the magician might be a mind reader as well. Careful to keep her smile intact, she forced herself to laugh off his comment.

"I just don't think it's nice to brag," she responded playfully.

"Chicken," he taunted in an equally playful tone as he made his way toward the party room door.

Despite the uneasy feeling he'd discovered more about her in three minutes than most men did in three years, she wished he'd stayed to chat a few minutes more.

Andi Burke, wearing one of the new, hot-pink Creative Cupcakes bibbed aprons, came in from the kitchen and stared at the cupcake mess on the floor. "What happened here?"

"Zorro came in, gave me a panic attack, and the tray slipped out of my hands." Rachel grabbed a couple of paper towels and squatted down to scoop up the crumpled cake and splattered frosting before her OCD kitchen safety friend could comment further. "Don't worry, I'll take care of the mess."

"I should have told you Officer Lockwell hired a magician for his daughter's birthday party." Andi bent to help her, and when they stood back up, she asked, "Did you speak to Mike?"

Rachel nodded, her gaze on the connecting door to the party room as it opened, and Mike reappeared. Tipping his head toward them as he walked across the floor, he said, "Good afternoon, ladies."

Mike went out the front door, and Rachel hurried around the display case of cupcakes and crossed over to the shop's square, six-foot-high, street-side window. She leaned her head toward the glass and watched him take four three-by-three-foot black painted boxes out of the back of a van.

"You should go after him," Andi teased, her voice filled with amusement. "He's very handsome."

"How can you tell?" Rachel drew away from the window, afraid Mike might catch her spying on him. "He's got a black mask covering the upper half of his face. He could have sunken eyes, shaved eyebrows, and facial tattoos."

Andi laughed. "He doesn't, and I know you like guys with dark hair. He's not as tall as my Jake, but he's still got a great build."

"Better not let Jake hear you say that," Rachel retorted. "And how do you know he has a great build? The guy's wrapped in a cape."

"I've seen him before," Andi said. "Without the cape."

"Where?"

"His photo was in the newspaper two weeks ago," Andi confided. "The senior editor at the *Astoria Sun* assigned Jake to write an article on Mike Palmer's set models."

"What are you talking about?"

"Mike Palmer created the miniature model replica of the medieval city of Hilltop for the movie *Battle for Warrior Mountain* and worked on set pieces for many other movies filmed around Astoria. His structural designs are so intricate that when the camera zooms in close, it looks real."

Mike returned through the front door, wheeling in the black boxes on an orange dolly. Rachel caught her breath as he looked her way before proceeding toward the party room with his equipment. Did the masked man find her as intriguing as she found him?

Andi's younger sister, Kim, came in from the kitchen with a large tray of red velvet cupcakes with cherry–cream cheese frosting. The three of them together, with Andi's boyfriend, Jake Hartman, as their financial partner, had managed to open Creative Cupcakes a month and a half earlier.

"Who's he?" Kim asked. She placed the cupcakes on the marble counter and pointed toward the billowing black cape of the magician.

"Mike the Magnificent," Rachel said dreamily.

An Excerpt from

THE CUPCAKE DIARIES: TASTE OF ROMANCE

> All I really need is love, but a little chocolate now
> and then doesn't hurt!
>
> —**Charles Schulz**

FOCUS, KIM REPRIMANDED herself. *Keep to the task at hand and stop eavesdropping on other people's conversations.*

But she didn't need to hear the crack of the teenage boy's heart to feel his pain. Or to remember the last time she'd heard the wretched words "I'm leaving" spoken to her.

She tried to ignore the couple as she picked up the pastry bag filled with pink icing and continued to decorate the tops of the strawberry preserve cupcakes. However, the discussion between the high school boy and what she assumed to be his girlfriend kept her attentive.

"When will I see you again?" he asked.

Kim glanced toward them and leaned closer.

"I don't know," the girl replied.

The soft lilt in her accent thrust the familiarity of the conversation even deeper into Kim's soul.

"I'll be going to the university for two years," the girl continued. "Maybe we meet again after."

Not likely. Kim shook her head, and her stomach tightened. From past experience, she knew once the school year was over in June, most foreign students went home, never to return.

And left many broken hearts in their wake.

"Two years is a long time," the boy said.

Forever was even longer. Kim drew in a deep breath as the unmistakable catch in the poor boy's voice replayed again and again in her mind. And her heart.

How long were they going to stand there and torment her by reminding her of her parting four years earlier with Gavin, the Irish student she'd dated through college? Dropping the bag of icing on the Creative Cupcakes counter, she moved toward them.

"Can I help you?" Kim asked, pulling on a new pair of food handler's gloves.

"I'll have the white chocolate macadamia," the girl said, pointing to the cupcake she wanted in the glass display case.

The boy dug his hands into his pockets, counted the meager change he'd managed to withdraw, and turned five shades of red.

"None for me." His Adam's apple bobbed as he swallowed. "How much for hers?"

"You have to have one, too," the girl protested. "It's your birthday."

Kim took one look at his lost-for-words expression and said, "If today is your birthday, the cupcakes are free." She added, "For both you and your guest."

The teenager's face brightened. "Really?"

Kim nodded and removed the cupcakes the two lovebirds wanted from the display case. She even put a birthday candle on one of them, a heart on the other. Maybe the girl would come back for him. Or he would fly to Ireland for her. *Maybe.*

Her eyes stung, and she squeezed them shut for a brief second. When she opened them again, she set her jaw. Enough was enough. Now that they had their cupcakes, she could escape back into her work and forget about romance and relationships and every regrettable moment she'd ever wasted on love.

She didn't need it. Not like her older sister, Andi, who had recently lost her heart to Jake Hartman, their Creative Cupcakes financier and reporter for the *Astoria Sun*. Or like her other co-owner friend, Rachel, who had just gotten engaged to Mike Palmer, a miniature model maker for movies who also doubled as the driver of their Cupcake Mobile.

All she needed was to dive deep into her desire to put paint on canvas. She glanced at the walls of the cupcake shop, adorned with her scenic oil, acrylic, and watercolor paintings. Maybe if she worked hard enough, she'd have the money to open her own art gallery, and she wouldn't need to decorate cupcakes anymore.

But for now, she needed to serve the next customer. *Where was Rachel?*

"Hi, Kim." Officer Ian Lockwell, one of their biggest supporters, sat on one of the stools lining the marble cupcake counter. "I'm wondering if you have the back party room available on June 27?"

Kim reached under the counter and pulled out the three-ring binder she, Andi, and Rachel had dubbed the Cupcake Diary to keep track of all things cupcake related. Looking at the calendar, she said, "Yes, the date is open. What's the occasion?"

"My wife and I have been married almost fifteen years," the big, square-jawed cop told her. "We're planning on renewing our vows on our anniversary and need a place to celebrate with friends and family."

"No better place to celebrate love than Creative Cupcakes," Kim assured him, glancing around at all the couples in the shop. "I'll put you on the schedule."

Next, the door opened, and a stream of romance writers filed in for their weekly meeting. Kim pressed her lips together. The group intimidated her with their watchful eyes and poised pens. They scribbled in their notebooks whenever she walked by as if writing down her every move, and she didn't want to give them any useful fodder. She hoped Rachel could take their orders, if she could find her.

"Rachel?"

No answer, but the phone rang—a welcome distraction. She picked up and said, "Creative Cupcakes, this is Kim."

"What are you doing there? I thought you were going to take time off."

Kim pushed into the privacy of the kitchen, glad it was Andi and not another customer despite the impending lecture tone. "I still have several dozen cupcakes to decorate."

"Isn't Rachel there with you?"

The door of the walk-in pantry burst open, and Rachel and Mike emerged, wrapped in each other's arms, laughing and grinning.

Kim rolled her eyes. "Yes, Rachel's here."

Rachel extracted herself from Mike's embrace and mouthed the word "sorry."

But Kim knew she wasn't. Rachel had been in her own red-headed, happy bubble ever since macho, dark-haired Mike the Magnificent had proposed two weeks earlier.

"I'll be in for my shift as soon as I get Mia off to afternoon kindergarten," Andi continued, "and the shop's way ahead in sales. There's no reason you can't take a break. Ever since you broke up with Gavin, you've become a workaholic."

Kim sucked in her breath at the mention of his name. Only Andi dared to ever bring him up.

"Gavin has nothing to do with my work."

"You never date."

"I'm concentrating on my career."

"It's been years since you've been out with anyone. You need to slow down, take time to smell the roses."

"Smell the roses?" Kim gasped. "Are you *serious*?"

"Go on an adventure," Andi amended.

"Working is an adventure."

"You used to dream of a different kind of adventure," Andi said, lowering her voice. "The kind that requires a passport."

Kim wished she'd never picked up the phone. Just because her sister had her life put back together didn't mean she had the right to tell her how to live.

"Painting cupcakes and canvas is the only adventure I need right now. I promised Dad I'd have the money to pay him for my new art easel by the end of the week."

"Dad doesn't care about the money, but he does care about you. He asked me to call."

"He did?" Kim stopped in front of the sink and rubbed her temples with her fingertips. Her sister was known to overreact, but their father? He didn't voice concern unless it was legitimate.

With the phone to her ear, she returned to the front counter of the couple-filled cupcake shop, her heart screaming louder and louder with each consecutive beat.

They were *everywhere*. By the window, at the tables, next to the display case. Couples, couples, couples. Everyone had a partner, had someone.

Almost everyone.

Instead of Goonies Day, the celebration of the 1985 release date of *The Goonies* movie, which was filmed in Astoria, she would have thought the calendar had been flipped back to Valentine's Day at Creative Cupcakes. And in her opinion, one Valentine's Day a year was more than enough.

She reached a hand into the pocket of her pink apron

and clenched the golden wings she had received on her first airplane flight as a child. The pin never left her side, and like the flying squirrel tattooed on her shoulder, it reminded her of her dream to fly, if not to another land, then at least to the farthest reaches of her imagination.

Where her heart would be free.

Okay, maybe she *did* spend too much time at the cupcake shop. "Tell Dad not to worry," Kim said into the phone. "Tell him . . . I'm taking the afternoon off."

"Promise?" Andi persisted.

Oh, yeah. Tearing off her apron, she turned around and threw it over Rachel's and Mike's heads. "I'm heading out the door now."

Acknowledgments

I WOULD LIKE to thank my editors, Lucia Macro and May Chen, and everyone else at Avon Impulse for their continued support, and also my new agent, Nicole Resciniti, for cheering me on and lending her guidance. You have all made this a wonderful experience.

About the Author

DARLENE PANZERA writes sweet, fun-loving romance and is a member of the Romance Writers of America's Greater Seattle and Peninsula chapters. Her career launched when her novella *The Bet* was picked by Avon Books and *New York Times* bestselling author Debbie Macomber to be published within Debbie's own novel, *Family Affair*. Darlene says, "I love writing stories that help inspire people to laugh, value relationships, and pursue their dreams."

Born and raised in New Jersey, Darlene is now a resident of the Pacific Northwest, where she lives with her husband and three children. When not writing she enjoys spending time with her family and her two horses, and loves camping, hiking, photography, and lazy days at the lake.

Join her on Facebook or at www.darlenepanzera.com.

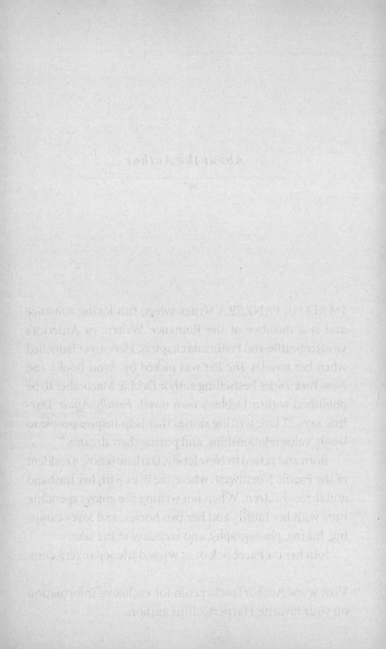

About the Author

DARLENE PANZERA's series sweet, fun-loving romance and is a member of the Romance Writers of America's Greater Seattle and Peninsula chapters. Her career launched when her novella *The Bet* was picked by Avon Books and *New York Times* bestselling author Debbie Macomber to be published within Debbie's own novel, *Family Affair*. Darlene says, "I love writing stories that help inspire people to laugh, value relationships, and pursue their dreams."

Born and raised in New Jersey, Darlene is now a resident of the Pacific Northwest, where she lives with her husband and three children. When not writing she enjoys spending time with her family, and her two horses, and loves camping, hiking, photography, and lazy days at the lake.

Join her on Facebook or at www.darlenepanzera.com.

Visit www.AuthorTracker.com for exclusive information on your favorite HarperCollins authors.

Give in to your impulses . . .
Read on for a sneak peek at four brand-new
e-book original tales of romance
from Avon Books.
Available now wherever e-books are sold.

RESCUED BY A STRANGER
By Lizbeth Selvig

CHASING MORGAN
BOOK FOUR: THE HUNTED SERIES
By Jennifer Ryan

THROWING HEAT
A DIAMONDS AND DUGOUTS NOVEL
By Jennifer Seasons

PRIVATE RESEARCH
AN EROTIC NOVELLA
By Sabrina Darby

An Excerpt from

RESCUED BY A STRANGER

by Lizbeth Selvig

When a stranger arrives in town on a vintage motorcycle, Jill Carpenter has no idea her life is about to change forever. She never expected that her own personal knight in shining armor would be an incredibly charming and handsome southern man—but one with a deep secret. When Jill's dreams of becoming an Olympic equestrian start coming true, Chase's past finally returns to haunt him. Can they get beyond dreams to find the love that will rescue their two hearts? Find out in the follow-up to *The Rancher and the Rock Star.*

"Angel?" Jill called. "C'mon, girl. Let's go get you something to eat." She'd responded to her new name all evening. Jill frowned.

Chase gave a soft, staccato, dog-calling whistle. Angel stuck her head out from a stall a third of the way down the aisle. "There she is. C'mon, girl."

Angel disappeared into the stall.

"Weird," Jill said, heading down the aisle.

At the door to a freshly bedded empty stall, they found Angel curled beside a mound of sweet, fragrant hay, staring up as if expecting them.

"Silly girl," Jill said. "You don't have to stay here. We're taking you home. Come."

Angel didn't budge. She rested her head between her paws and gazed through raised doggy brows. Chase led the way into the stall. "Everything all right, pup?" He stroked her head.

Jill reached for the dog, too, and her hand landed on Chase's. They both froze. Slowly he rotated his palm and wove his fingers through hers. The few minor fireworks she'd felt in the car earlier were nothing compared to the explosion now detonating up her arm and down her back.

"I've been trying to avoid this since I got off that dang horse." His voice cracked into a low whisper.

"Why?"

He stood and pulled her to her feet. "Because I am not a guy someone as young and good as you are should let do this."

"You've saved my life and rescued a dog. Are you trying to tell me I should be *worried* about you?"

She touched his face, bold enough in the dark to do what light had made her too shy to try.

"Maybe."

The hard, smooth fingertips of his free hand slid inexorably up her forearm and covered the hand on his cheek. Drawing it down to his side, he pulled her whole body close, and the little twister of excitement in her stomach burst into a thousand quicksilver thrills. Her eyelids slipped closed, and his next question touched them in warm puffs of breath.

"If I were to kiss you right now, would it be too soon?"

Her eyes flew open, and she searched his shadowy gaze, incredulous. "You're asking permission? Who does that?"

"Seemed like the right thing."

"Well, permission granted. Now hush."

She freed her hands, placed them on his cheeks, roughened with beard stubble, and rose on tiptoe to meet his mouth while he gripped the back of her head.

The soft kiss nearly knocked her breathless. Chase dropped more hot kisses on each corner of her mouth and down her chin, feathered her nose and her cheeks, and finally returned to her mouth. Again and again he plied her bottom lip with his teeth, stunning her with his insistent exploration. The pressure of his lips and the clean, masculine scent of his skin took away her equilibrium. She could only follow the motions of his head and revel in the heat stoking the fire in her belly.

He pulled away at last and pressed parted lips to her forehead.

An Excerpt from

CHASING MORGAN
Book Four: The Hunted Series
by Jennifer Ryan

Morgan Standish can see things other people can't. She can see the past and future. These hidden gifts have prevented her from getting close to anyone—except FBI agent Tyler Reed. Morgan is connected to him in a way even she can't explain. She's solved several cases for him in the past, but will her gifts be enough to bring down a serial killer whose ultimate goal is to kill her? Find out in Book Four of The Hunted Series.

Morgan's fingers flew across the laptop keyboard propped on her knees. She took a deep breath, cleared her mind, and looked out past her pink-painted toes resting on the railing and across her yard to the densely wooded area at the edge of her property. Her mind's eye found her guest winding his way through the trees. She still had time before Jack stepped out of the woods separating her land from his. She couldn't wait to meet him.

Images, knowings, they just came to her. She'd accepted that part of herself a long time ago. As she got older, she'd learned to use her gift to seek out answers.

She finished her buy-and-sell orders and switched from her day trading page to check her psychic website and read the questions submitted by customers. She answered several quickly, letting the others settle in her mind until the answers came to her.

One stood out. The innocuous question about getting a job held an eerie vibe.

The familiar strange pulsation came over her. The world disappeared, as though a door had slammed on reality. The images came to her like hammer blows, one right after the other, and she took the onslaught, knowing something important needed to be seen and understood.

An older woman lying in a bed, hooked up to a machine feeding her medication. Frail and ill, she had translucent skin and dark circles marring her tortured eyes. Her pain washed over Morgan like a tsunami.

The woman yelled at someone, her face contorted into something mean and hateful. An unhappy woman—one who'd spent her whole life blaming others and trying to make them as miserable as she was.

A pristine white pillow floating down, inciting panic, amplified to terror when it covered the woman's face, her frail body swallowed by the sheets.

Morgan had an overwhelming feeling of suffocation.

The woman tried desperately to suck in a breath, but couldn't. Unable to move her lethargic limbs, she lay petrified and helpless under his unyielding hands. Lights flashed on her closed eyelids.

Death came calling.

A man stood next to the bed, holding the pillow like a shield. His mouth opened on a contorted, evil, hysterical laugh that rang in her ears and made her skin crawl. She squeezed her eyes closed to blot out his malevolent image and thoughts.

Murderer!

The word rang in her head as the terrifying emotions overtook her.

Morgan threw up a wall in her mind, blocking the cascade of disturbing pictures and feelings. She took several deep breaths and concentrated on the white roses growing in profusion just below the porch railing. Their sweet fragrance filled the air. With every breath, she centered herself and found her inner calm, pushing out the anger and rage left over from the vision. Her body felt like a lead weight, lightening as her energy came back. The drowsiness faded with each new breath. She'd be fine in a few minutes.

The man on horseback emerged from the trees, coming toward her home. Her guest had arrived.

Focused on the computer screen, she slowly and meticulously typed her answer to the man who had asked about a job and inadvertently opened himself up to telling her who he really was at heart.

She replied simply:

You'll get the job, but you can't hide from what you did.
You need help. Turn yourself in to the police.

An Excerpt from

THROWING HEAT
A Diamonds and Dugouts Novel

by Jennifer Seasons

Nightclub manager Leslie Cutter has never
been one to back down from a bet. So when
Peter Kowalskin, pitcher for the Denver
Rush baseball team, bets her that she can't
keep her hands off of him, she's not about
to let the arrogant, gorgeous playboy win.
But as things heat up, this combustible pair
will have to decide just how much they're
willing to wager on one another . . . and on
a future that just might last forever.

"Is there something you want?" he demanded with a raised eyebrow, amused at being able to throw her words right back at her.

"You wish," Leslie retorted and tossed him a dismissive glance. Only he caught the gleam of interest in her eyes and knew her for the liar that she was.

Peter took a step toward her, closing the gap by a good foot until only an arm's reach separated them. He leaned forward and caged her in by placing a hand on each armrest of her chair. Her eyes widened the tiniest bit, but she held her ground.

"I wish many, many things."

"Really?" she questioned and shifted slightly away from him in her chair. "Such as what?"

Peter couldn't help noticing that her breathing had gone

shallow. How about that? "I wish to win the World Series this season." It would be a hell of a way to go out.

Her gaze landed on his mouth and flicked away. "Boring."

Humor sparked inside him at that, and he chuckled. "You want exciting?"

She shrugged. "Why not? Amuse me."

That worked for him. Hell yeah. If she didn't watch herself, he was going to excite the pants right off of her.

Just excitement, arousal, and sexual pleasure. That was what he was looking for this time around. And it was going to be fun leading her up to it.

But if he wanted her there, then he had to start.

Pushing until he'd tipped her chair back and only the balls of her feet were on the desk, her painted toes curling for a grip, Peter lowered his head until his mouth was against her ear. She smelled like coconut again, and his gut went tight.

"I wish I had you bent over this desk right here with your hot bare ass in the air."

She made a small sound in her throat and replied, "Less boring."

Peter grinned. Christ, the woman was tough. "Do you remember what I did to you that night in Miami? The thing that made you come hard, twice—one on top of the other?" He sure as hell did. It had involved his tongue, his fingers, and Leslie on all fours with her face buried in a pillow, moaning his name like she was begging for deliverance.

She tried to cover it, but he heard her quick intake of breath. "It wasn't that memorable."

Bullshit.

He slid a hand from the armrest and squeezed the top of her right leg, his thumb rubbing lazily back and forth on the skin of her inner thigh. Her muscles tensed, but she didn't pull away.

"Need a reminder?"

An Excerpt from

PRIVATE RESEARCH
An Erotic Novella
by Sabrina Darby

The last person Mina Cavallari expects to
encounter in the depths of the National
Archives while doing research on a thesis is
Sebastian Graham, an outrageously sexy financial
whiz. Sebastian is conducting a little research of
his own into the history of what he thinks is just
another London underworld myth, the fabled
Harridan House. When he discovers that the
private sex club still exists, he convinces Mina
to join him on an odyssey into the intricacies of
desire, pleasure, and, most surprisingly of all, love.

It was the most innocuous of sentences: "A cappuccino, please." Three words—without a verb to ground them, even. Yet, at the sound, my hand stilled mid-motion, my own paper coffee cup paused halfway between table and mouth. I looked over to the counter of the cafe. It was mid-afternoon, quieter than it had been when I'd come in earlier for a quick lunch, and only three people were in line behind the tall, slim-hipped, blond-haired man whose curve of shoulder and loose-limbed stance struck a chord in me as clearly as his voice.

Of course it couldn't be. In two years, surely, I had forgotten the exact tenor of his voice, was now confusing some other deep, posh English accent with his. Yet I watched the man, waited for him to turn around, as if there were any significant chance that in a city of eight million people, during the middle of the business day, I'd run into the one English acquaintance I had. At the National Archives, no less.

At the first glimpse of his profile, I sucked in my breath sharply, nearly dropping my coffee. Then he turned fully, looking around, likely for the counter with napkins and sugar. I watched his gaze pass over me and then snap back in recognition. I was both pleased and terrified. I'd come to London to put the past behind me, not to face down my demons. I'd been doing rather well these last months, but maybe this was part of some cosmic plan. As my time in England wound down, in order to move forward with my life, I had to come face to face with Sebastian Graham again.

"Mina!" He had an impressive way of making his voice heard across a room without shouting, and as he walked toward me, I put my cup down and stood, all too aware that while he looked like a fashionable professional about town, I still looked like a grad student––no makeup, hair pulled back in a ponytail, wearing jeans, sneakers, and a sweater.

"This is a pleasant surprise. Research for your dissertation? Anne Gracechurch, right?"

I nodded, bemused that he remembered a detail from what had surely been a throwaway conversation two years earlier. But of course I really shouldn't have been. Seb was brilliant, and brilliance wasn't the sort of thing that just faded away.

Neither, apparently, was his ability to make my pulse beat a bit faster or to tie up my tongue for a few seconds before I found my stride. He wasn't traditionally handsome, at least not in an American way. Too lean, too angular, hair receding a bit at the temples, and I was fairly certain he was now just shy of thirty. But I'd found him attractive from the first moment I'd met him.

I still did.

"That's right. What are you doing here? I mean, at the Archives."

"Ah." He shifted and smiled at me, and there was something about that smile that felt wicked and secretive. "A small genealogical project. Mind if I join you?"

I shook my head and sat back down. He pulled out his chair and sat, too, folding his long legs one over the other. Why was that sexy to me?

I focused on his face. He was pale. Much paler than he'd been in New Jersey, like he now spent most of his time indoors. Which should have been a turn-off. Yet, despite everything, I sat there imagining him in the kitchen of my apartment wearing nothing but boxer shorts. Apparently my memory was as good as his.

And I still remembered the crushing humiliation and disappointment of that last time we'd talked.